jon talton

CONCRETE DESERT

thomas dunne books
st. martin's minotaur
new york

THOMAS DUNNE BOOKS.
An imprint of St. Martin's Press.

www.minotaurbooks.com

Designed by Lorelle Graffeo

Library of Congress Cataloging-in-Publication Data

Talton, Jon.
Concrete desert / Jon Talton — 1st ed.
p. cm.
ISBN 0-312-26953-6
1. History teachers—Fiction. 2. Phoenix (Ariz.)—Fiction.
3. Unemployed—Fiction. I. Title.

PS3620.A58 C66 2001
813'.6—dc21 2001019257

10 9 8 7 6 5 4 3 2

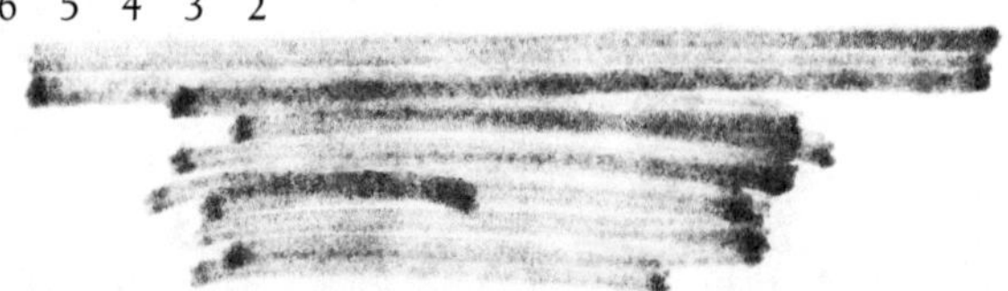

for susan

acknowledgments

Many people made *Concrete Desert* a reality. I am especially grateful to Ruth Cavin, my editor at St. Martin's Press, for her perfect pitch and graceful guidance. Also at St. Martin's, Julie Sullivan and Linda McFall provided indispensable help. My agent, Jay Poyner, was a rock of good counsel. I am in debt to many friends and colleagues, particularly Kathleen Doane and Diane Suchetka, fine writers and givers of creative first aid. Susan Moore, the novel's fiercest supporter, also decided to marry the author, and for her I am most grateful.

CONCRETE
DESERT

The storms don't come into the city anymore. When I was a little boy, when we had evaporative cooling and Kennedy was president, the late-summer monsoons swept into Arizona from the Sea of Cortez and cooled Phoenix with wind and rain. Now the city has become a concrete slab eighty miles across and the weather has changed. Most times, we can only see the clouds hovering out beyond the mountains, dropping precious rain on the desert, tantalizing us with lightning, leaving us with dust.

It was July. High summer in Phoenix, when a temperature of 105 degrees is a relief and workaday guys in traffic jams can turn into killers if they get into a fender bender. It's the time of year when the asphalt gets so hot, it can leave second-degree burns on your skin; when $350-a-night resorts hold half-price sales, and everybody who can afford it heads to the ocean; when the air-conditioning of 3 million people pushes the power grid to the edge of a shutdown and a headline about a dozen illegal immigrants suffocating in a locked tractor-trailer brings a resigned shrug. My hometown.

I had been back in Phoenix for exactly six weeks, back in the house that had belonged to my grandparents, the house where I grew up. It was a small Spanish Mediterranean two blocks west of Central on Cypress Avenue, surrounded by oleander hedges, orange trees, and palms. Grandfather built the house in 1924. During the years I was gone, the city had taken to calling the area the Willo Historic District. When I was a kid, it was just a neighborhood and everybody knew everybody else. Now my grandparents had been dead for years, and the families that lived nearby had moved away. The neighborhood was supposed to be popular with young professionals. I hoped so. I needed to sell the house and find a new job.

It was a Sunday evening, the worst time of the week to be alone. Ellington was on the CD player, the 1956 Newport concert. I was about half a martini away from loose ends when the wind started to unsettle the palm trees outside the big picture window and the doorbell rang. Maybe I'd been a little isolated for those six weeks, but it occurred to me that I hadn't heard the doorbell for years, at least since Grandmother was still alive. The deep clang put a stake of dread in me that usually comes with late-night phone calls. Then I opened the door and saw a ghost.

"David Mapstone!" The ghost knew my name and rushed to give me a hug. At five feet five, she could fit completely inside my arms and have the top of her head nestle under my chin. Once upon a time, her name had been Julie Riding, my first lover.

I blathered the nervous small talk of unexpected reunions and invited her inside. In the high-ceilinged living room, she sat in one of the leather chairs that face the picture window and accepted my offer of a drink—scotch, neat. I poured her a couple of fingers of McClelland's and then sat opposite her in the other chair with my glass of Bombay Sapphire.

"I can't believe you're back in town," she was saying in a bright alto chirp. She wore a short summer dress that was a little too young for her. But she still had damn nice legs and she knew it. Her hair was a couple of shades darker than the honey color that I remembered, and it was shorter now, businesslike, above the shoulders. Time was beginning to cut itself into the skin around her eyes, but they were still the darkest blue I had ever seen, the color of the dusk sky in the mountains. She was saying how little the house had changed, how she was sorry to hear about my grandmother's death a few years before, how she'd tried to keep up with my teaching career after I left town.

Then she turned red and downed the scotch in one gulp. I refilled her glass, and she didn't stop me.

"Shit," she said, the chirp gone from her voice. "I rehearsed this speech a few hundred times, but I know it sounds forced. I know how strange it seems for me just to show up suddenly, when I walked out the way I did. Now, here I am. Wanting something."

I filed that away. "I just thought you'd been held up a really long time in the ladies' room."

"David, it's been twenty years."

My head is always full of dates—1066, 1492, 1789, 1914. It's an occupational hazard when you teach history. The last time I saw Julie Riding was just before Christmas 1979, when she sat across from me in a dark little bar near the university and said she didn't want to see me anymore. She was in love with someone else, she said. He was older and—let me remember this right—"was a real world-beater," which I took to mean he had money. I was just a college student with a smoky old convertible.

For months after that, amid various stages of anger and hurt, I imagined the life Julie was living without me—I have a very vivid imagination—and what I would say and do if she ever came back. But as my life began to change, she faded from my thoughts, until the years pushed her into that fond drawer of occasional memory reserved for first lovers. Now she was here in my living room and part of me was feeling odd, but another part was feeling as if she'd been gone about twenty minutes. Mostly, I was just glad for the company.

"Do you mind?" She produced a Marlboro Light from her purse. I shook my head. She lit it and took a drag that sounded soothing even from where I was sitting. "I'm seriously addicted," she said.

We sat in silence awhile, watching the clouds and wind flow in from the east; then a curtain of dust began to fall out of the sky. I leaned forward and just let her find her words. She played with her hair, pushing it back. She'd always done that.

"God, you look great," she said finally. I was wearing jeans and a white polo shirt, nothing special. "No, I mean it. It's like you've really grown into your face. You're going to be a hell of a good-looking middle-aged man."

"Thanks, I think," I said.

"Our birthdays are two weeks apart, remember?" She sipped her scotch and gave me a sly smile. "David, it's the strangest thing. I was at the Hard Rock Café with some girlfriends one night, and there was Mike Peralta at the bar. He wasn't in uniform, of course, and he looked like he was with some pretty high-powered people, but I just went over and gave him a hug, I mean, my God, it had been about as long as since I'd last seen you.

"Anyway, I asked about you, and Mike said you were back in Phoenix and working for the Sheriff's Office again. I knew I had to see you, so here I am. My God, are you a deputy again? I thought that was just your youthful adventure."

She stubbed out the butt and lit another, melting a little into the chair. "Deputy David Mapstone of the Old West." She giggled.

I smiled at her, glad to provide amusement for an old girlfriend. Some people decide at age fourteen that they're going to be accountants, and that's all they do for their whole lives. My résumé is a little more complicated. Especially after this summer.

"I'm just doing a little consulting. Researching some old cases for Peralta. I'm in between jobs."

"So you're not teaching?" she asked. "Your great dream was to be a history professor, I thought."

Since when do we get our great dreams? I thought, getting up to refresh our drinks. I said over my shoulder, "The tenure committee at San Diego State didn't like me, and there are too many people with Ph.D.'s in history, anyway. Something will come up."

She followed me into the kitchen. "When did you start drinking martinis?"

"When I was married to a millionaire's daughter."

"Dorothy Parker said martinis lead to all sorts of sexual misjudgments," Julie said absently, then added, "What was her name?"

"Dorothy Parker?"

"Your ex-wife, you goof."

"Patty," I said.

"Good boomer name," Julie said. "All those fathers in lust with Patti Page. Kids?"

"No."

"And you've been divorced about a year?"

"Mmmhmm."

"I can tell it in your voice," she said. She wasn't wearing a wedding ring. I looked out the window at the garden courtyard, where a palm tree was dancing slowly in the wind. We weren't going to get any rain. Julie Riding in my kitchen, talking about my divorce. "Tell me about you."

"What's to tell?" She smiled. "Life goes on. I'm divorced. My daughter's fourteen, and she just made cheerleader. I'm in marketing at the Phoenician resort, and I work all the time." She made it sound like a neat package.

Finally, she asked, "Do you remember my little sister? Phaedra."

Now we were down to the "wanting something" part of the evening.

I said I remembered an eight-year-old kid.

Truth was, I barely remembered her sister at all. A skinny kid with red hair who played the cello and had an odd name. She was in the background one night when Julie took me home to meet her parents, and they all had a big fight. Mostly, I remembered her name, Phaedra. Not a popular boomer name.

"She's twenty-eight now, David," Julie said. "And she's missing."

"Have you been to the cops?" I asked.

"Yeah, they took a report. What does that mean? They told me she was an adult and that unless there was some indication of foul play, there wasn't much they could do."

"So what can I do?"

"I know you have friends in the Sheriff's Office. Even if you're just a consultant. Maybe you could ask around?" The blue eyes implored. "It's been two weeks since she was supposed to come over for dinner. I haven't had a call, nothing. Her apartment hasn't been slept in."

"New boyfriend?"

"That's never made her drop off the face of the earth."

"What about her job?"

She shook her head. "Phaedra was kind of in between careers. She was working at a photo studio. She had a lot of gifts, but she never did well playing the game at work, you know what I mean?"

As a matter of fact, I did. I asked, "Do you have any reason to suspect something bad has happened to her?"

Julie paused and the tip of her cigarette glowed contemplatively. "This is a very dangerous city, and she's a pretty young woman. What more do you need?"

I promised to ask some questions around the Sheriff's Office. Julie smashed out the cigarette, and it was time to leave. I walked her out to her car. The storm had blown through, and the night was dusty, hot, and expectant.

"You're back in time for the monsoon season," she said, aiming her key chain at a silver Lexus, which beeped attentively.

"You're down in the barrio now," she said.

"I guess. I haven't lived in this house for a long time."

"It's all coming back down here," she said, starting up the car. "Close-in city living."

I watched her drive her car to the end of the block and disappear around the corner. I didn't care about Julie Riding, and I didn't want to start.

Chapter 2

Maricopa County Chief Deputy Mike Peralta, all six feet six inches and 250 pounds of him, bulled his way through the corridor, trailing reporters like a contrail behind a big jet. "No," he was saying. "You'll have to talk to the sheriff. . . . He'll issue a statement. . . . He'll be available for interviews." Half a dozen voices made demands that he ignored.

"Mapstone." He zeroed in on me and, wrapping a massive arm around my shoulders, turned me around and pushed me through the private side door into his office suite. I could feel the 9-mm Glock semiautomatic in the shoulder rig under his suit.

"Goddamn media jackals," he said distastefully.

"When have you ever met publicity you didn't like?" I said.

He looked at me sourly. "All they want to talk about is the chain gang or the tent jail or the latest goat fuck with some politician, and the sheriff's the one who speaks for the department on that."

"That's what happens when you work for 'America's toughest sheriff.' "

Peralta ignored me, dropped into his big desk chair, leaned back, and settled his feet on an otherwise-immaculate desktop. He wore a tan summer suit atop nicely tooled black lizard boots. When it suited his mood, he also wore an expensive Stetson. His face was a bit broader and darker than when I'd first met him, but otherwise, he had hardly aged in the twenty years I'd known him.

He pointed toward a thick folder on the table behind me. He didn't offer a chair. I sat anyway and hefted the folder onto my lap.

"You'll like this one," he said, rubbing an imaginary beard. "Rebecca Stokes. Twenty-one years old, comes home on the train, takes a taxi to her apartment, pays the driver, and is never seen alive again."

"I've heard of this one. My grandparents talked about it when I was growing up."

"It was 1959," he said. The year I was born. "She turned up in the desert two weeks later, body dump. That was the strange thing about those old murders in Phoenix: No matter where they got dumped in the desert—and this was a small town surrounded by hundreds of miles of nothing—somebody always found them.

"Anyway, see what you can give me on it by the time I have the regular press briefing this Thursday." He popped a can of diet Coke and took a deep swig.

"You're enjoying this too damned much," I said.

"What? It took you three days to turn up the new evidence that nailed the Samuels case. Fifteen-year-old case and it takes you three days."

"That was lucky—connect the dots."

"That was a week's worth of headlines for the department." Peralta smiled. "And a nice thousand bucks for you. You know the drill—dig up something I can use and you get paid as a private contractor, and you act as a volunteer posse deputy. If I can't get you back into the department one way, I can try another way."

"I'm grateful for the work, Mike, but it's all temporary," I said. "I don't even know if I'm going to stay in Phoenix."

"Forget that college shit," Peralta said. "No way they're going to give tenure to a middle-aged white male former cop—who's from Barry Goldwater's home state no less."

"I'm not middle-aged. And actually, the tenure committee said I was 'unwilling to abandon my Western intellectual outlook' and become more sensitive to 'nonlinearity.' "

"Fuck me blind and call me Susie," Peralta said. "I knew you'd never fit in with those Commies. Teaching rich kids to hate their country, God, and their parents."

"I'm teaching still," I said halfheartedly.

"One course in American history for some morons and blue-hairs at the junior college," he snorted. "Hell, maybe I'll sign up. Let you teach me something."

"That would be a first," I said.

The phone rang and he grabbed it harshly, saying "Peralta" before the receiver reached his head. It was his habit, strange to listen to when you were calling. His heavy brow darkened by several degrees—I had seen his mood shift this suddenly many times when Peralta and I were partners years before, and it never ceased to make me uneasy. "Yeah. . . . Shit. . . ." I heard his end of the conversation. "Bullshit! . . . That's the county supervisors' problem, not ours. . . . Goddamned right—they made the mess, not us. Bullshit, we're buying the Jimmys. Do it." He slammed the phone back into its cradle.

"I've got six prostitutes dead over the past three months." He thumped a set of files on his desk. "I've got half the Lake Pleasant substation called in sick next shift. Fucking titty-bar owner Bobby Hamid's one step ahead of a court order. Crips terrorizing the white folks in Litchfield Park. A million-dollar burglary out in Cave Creek—and what do I get to deal with? The goddamned departmental budget. The goddamned county supervisors! Seventh-largest county in the United States, and they run it like some little town in Alabama."

The first time I ever saw Mike Peralta, he was teaching martial arts at the Sheriff's Academy, and I was a twenty-year-old cadet. I wanted to save the world with a badge. But I also thought I was pretty damned smart, with my new B.A. degree in history. He took me down so hard, my head rang for two days. Soon after, he was the five-year veteran who broke me in as a rookie when we were patrolling the no-man's-land between Scottsdale and Tempe. We worked apart for two years while he was trying out jail administration and I was getting my master's degree. Then we partnered again in the east county as it became clear I was going to be a teacher, not a cop. Now here he was in the big office, the number-two guy in the department. I wish I could truthfully say I knew him.

He sighed, leaned back in his big chair, and really saw me for the first time. I was wearing a loose white cotton shirt and chinos—"goddamned J. Crew preppy shit," Peralta had called it, to show he disapproved.

"Put on your ID card," he ordered. "It's policy. You may be ashamed of being here, but you're a sworn deputy like every other swinging dick on Madison Street, and we all have to wear our ID cards." I pulled it out and clipped it on my shirt. "Deputy Sheriff," it said, and there I was in a picture, looking not too different from the way I did on my old faculty identification card, with one difference—my beard was gone. The picture would show you I have large, gentle brown eyes and wavy dark hair that women sometimes like, and roundish, undefined facial bones that they don't.

The picture wouldn't show you that I'm a little over six foot one—short in the NBA—and I have the broad shoulders and wide stride that helped me cool off tough guys when I was a cop.

"So what do you want?" Peralta demanded.

I told him about Phaedra Riding as he swung his chair back and forth in a slow arc. It was maddening if you didn't know him, but it was just Peralta. "You pull the incident report?"

I slid it across the desk, and he studied it.

"Julie Riding," he mumbled. "Where do I know that name? Hey, this is Julie, your Julie," he said, brightening. "I mean she's the complainant—it's her sister. Jeez."

"That's what I thought when she showed up at my door last night."

"I ran into her a couple of weeks ago, and she asked about you," Peralta said. "She's still a fox. I never understood how you lucked into that."

"She left me, as I recall."

Peralta grunted and went back to the report. I looked around his office; the walls always held some new award or photograph. Peralta with Goldwater. Peralta on horseback with the sheriff. Peralta in SWAT uniform during the killings at the Buddhist temple years before. Peralta in a tux with the business muckety-mucks of the Phoenix 40. Peralta with the Suns at the Western Conference Championships.

"Weird name," he said finally. "How do you say it?"

"Feed-ra or Fade-ra," I said, pronouncing it. "Like Phoenix."

"Weird," he said. "Sounds like some made-up hippie bullshit name."

"Phaedra was the daughter of Minos," I started to explain but his eyes immediately glazed. "Greek mythology . . ." God, I had been out of the cop world too long.

"Sounds like a head case to me," he said finally. "Artsy-fartsy little rich girl head case. She'll turn up. Probably schtupping some new guy."

"No Jane Does who fit this description turn up lately?" I asked.

"You're a deputy sheriff," he said. "Go do some police work. You remember how? Or did all those years trying to pick up college trim ruin your brain?"

"Fuck you," I said. It was our repartee, harmless for now. "I'm a part-time contract employee, a researcher, and if I get some information on old murder cases, it's all gravy to you and the sheriff. You know if I go to Missing Persons, I'll get a whole different reception than if you call the commanding officer and make an inquiry."

Peralta sighed and picked up the phone. "Dominguez? Peralta. Remember my old partner Dave Mapstone? Yeah, the professor. He's back in town, working for us part-time. He's interested in nine nine-two oh one three four five, Phaedra Riding? *Ph,* yeah, like Phoenix. Anything new? What'd we do? . . . Yeah, yeah, I know you've got people pulled in to work the Harquahala thing. . . . Okay."

He turned to me. "They don't know shit. You know how these missing persons cases go. She's an adult. No evidence of a crime. We have no reason to suspect foul play. Does Julie suspect foul play?" I shook my head. "What about her car?"

"Blue Nissan," I said. "I checked the impound lists, the hot sheets, nothing."

"So it sits," Peralta said. "She'll turn up."

"So you don't mind if I do some checking?"

"Not as long as you do your work for me first. And you don't get in some jurisdictional cluster fuck with Phoenix PD. What? You trying to score some points with Julie, rekindle the flame?"

"We've both moved on," I said, standing up to leave. "I'm just helping an old friend."

"Yeah, right," he said, crumpling the diet Coke can and tossing it through a Phoenix Suns basketball hoop into the trash can. "Sharon is on my back to have you over for dinner, y'know."

"I will," I said. Mike and his wife had invited me over a month ago.

"Then make it this Friday," he said, and turned his head toward his paperwork. I started out.

"You know who she's related to?"

I stopped and turned back to him. "Phaedra?"

"No, no, Stokes, Rebecca Stokes. She was the niece of John Henry McConnico."

"The former governor?" I said. He nodded. "So that would have made her—what, a first cousin to Brent McConnico?"

"The majority leader of the Arizona Senate," Peralta said. "He's seen as the next governor."

Peralta was always working the angles.

I crossed Jefferson Street against the light and made my way through César Chávez Plaza, deserted in the early-afternoon heat. It was one of those big sky–beautiful days in Phoenix, when the bare desert mountains in every direction were sharply defined by the intense light of the unencumbered sun. That same sun felt like a radiation gun on every exposed pore—the temperature was supposed to top 105 degrees today. A lone ragpicker started to hit me up for money but did a quick retreat when he saw my Sheriff's Office ID. I took the thing off and stuffed it into my pocket.

When I was twenty years old, that ID card and gold star had been my most prized possessions. They represented the law, the public trust—that was what Peralta said the first day I met him. It took four hard years to get it through my head that law enforcement wasn't for me. And yet, here I was. I could call this part-time, temporary, research, whatever. But I was carrying a badge again—and working for Mike Peralta.

The millions of dollars in computers at the main Sheriff's Administration Building were little help with a forty-year-old murder case, so I headed over to the old City Hall–County Courthouse, where forgotten records were stored in the attic. When Rebecca Stokes was murdered, this five-story burnt-brown building was where justice was dispensed in Maricopa County. When Rebecca Stokes was murdered, Eisenhower was president, trains still arrived at Union Station, and a small police force rarely had to deal with homicide.

Carl, the security guard, had spent thirty-five years with the Arizona Highway Patrol. But his perfect posture and fluffy, snow-white mustache reminded me of a retired British army officer. He spent fifteen minutes talking about how an arsonist was at work in his neighborhood, and how the easterners and Californians were ruining Phoenix. He showed me an article that said Phoenix was growing so fast that an acre of desert every hour was being swallowed up by the city. It was written by an old friend of mine, Lorie Pope at the *Republic.* The city had changed, gotten bigger, dirtier, and more dangerous. I didn't know whom to blame. Then Carl went away and left me alone in the musty, high-ceilinged clutter.

Sometimes, I feel like I've spent half my life in libraries, but this place was something else again. Historians dream of coming across old diaries from the Civil War in some attic, and this was my attic of treasures: fifty or sixty years of records from the city and county. I doubted if ten people even knew they were up here. It was like an overgrown vacant lot that, instead of being littered with old tires and washing machines, had accumulated decades of cast-off files as the old building went from its original use as a combined city-county building to being Phoenix Police Headquarters to finally housing a mishmash of government offices. There was no order to any of the hundreds of dusty cartons, rusty green and gray file cabinets, and rotting ledgers. But after a few trips, I had begun to find a few caches I might need someday.

I didn't know exactly what I was looking for, but whatever it was would begin to fill in some of the pieces about Rebecca Stokes. My ex-wife, Patty, told me that every woman has her secrets. My time in law enforcement had taught me that every case contains threads that nobody has the time or inclination to pull. I would be satisfied to find just one of them.

Peralta had some of the finest evidence technicians and detectives in the country to help him with a state-of-the art homicide investigation. I was here to "think outside the box," as he put it—he read too many business magazines. So I spent an hour reading the case file. Then I opened my old Mac PowerBook and began to make some notes.

What did I know? A twenty-one-year-old woman gets off a train at midnight and takes a cab home. Then she disappears and turns up dead. The file Peralta had given me said the body was in fairly good shape when it was found by a power-line crew. But the forensic techniques of 1959 were fairly primitive. The autopsy report had disappeared, but I did have a letter from the medical examiner, saying Rebecca died of strangulation, and noting that some residual bruises around the genitals and the presence of semen indicated sexual assault. She was naked except for a bra, and there were no fibers or hairs found on the body, nothing but the dust and burrs from the desert. No tire tracks, either.

The obvious suspect was the cabdriver. But the report and the attached news clippings said he was a decorated Phoenix cop who was working a second job driving a taxi. He voluntarily took a polygraph and passed. And that was it. No suspects were ever even questioned in the case.

Rebecca was what was called in the fifties a "career girl," well liked by her coworkers, no steady boyfriend. She'd come to Arizona to study at the state college—now Arizona State University—and took a job as a secretary in the law office of Larkin, Reading and Page. Now I also knew she was the niece of the governor—something the police reports and newspapers had omitted.

I found a carton with old radio logs from the late 1950s and paged through them. I wanted to know what else was going on in Phoenix when Stokes disappeared. An hour later, I didn't have much more than an appreciation for what a difference a mere four decades can make. The Phoenix of 1959 was less than a quarter of the size it is today—in many ways, it was just an overgrown farm town, although the postwar growth was at full throttle—and the police calls reflected it. It was a city with clear demarcations between "good" and "bad" parts of town. There were fights and disturbances in the Deuce—the old skid row, leveled years later to make room for the

Civic Plaza and America West Arena—and the poor Mexican-American neighborhoods, where I'm sure the police administered their own rough justice. But around Rebecca Stokes's apartment near the Phoenix Country Club on Thomas Road, life had seemed almost surreally safe. I thought of my own neighborhood at that time, neat and dull, where the night held only the fragrance of citrus blossoms and the sound of train whistles.

One thing did catch my eye. A week before Rebecca Stokes disappeared, PPD responded to a prowler call from a house two blocks away from her apartment. It wasn't much, but I needed a place to start. I made note of the officer's names. Maybe they were still alive, which was probably more than I could hope for the detective who had led the Stokes investigation.

I replaced the radio logs and crossed the room to a shelf containing old city directories and phone books. The 1959 city directory was missing, but I found 1960 and turned to the section that showed residents by address. I made note of the families and individuals living along her block and the street immediately to the south. All the lives, reduced to lines on old sheets of paper. I also checked the listings for the railroad, just to see if they listed a station agent or anybody in charge at Union Station, but I came up with nothing. But it gave me another idea, and I went back to the logs. Sure enough, a handful of police calls to Union Station yielded a complainant's name, J. T. Smith of the Southern Pacific.

I asked Carl if I could borrow his telephone and phone book. It was all a long shot, but I was motivated and wanted to have something to show Peralta, whose impatience was legendary. I checked the names from the city directory against the new phone book, a fool's errand in a city of transients. Sure enough, name after name led me nowhere. Forty years was ample time to die, move, or remarry. I made note of a J. T. Smith in Sun City, but odds were he wasn't my railroad man. Of all the leads it had to be a "Smith", I muttered to myself. Then I hit one: There was still a George Harvey listed on Twelfth Street, just around the corner from Rebecca Stokes's old apartment.

* * *

The area around the old North Phoenix High School had been one of the nicest in town back in the fifties. Now it was part of miles of declining east side neighborhoods marked by the stately palm trees of better times and the hieroglyphic gang graffiti of now. But the Harvey address belonged to a pleasant prewar home surrounded by lush oleanders and flowers. After the third knock, a small woman with uncombed white hair and a purple housedress pulled open the door and peered out at me. The house seemed totally dark behind her. I showed her my star and MCSO identification. She placed a wandlike object against her throat and invited me inside in a mechanical voice. "You don't have a cigarette, do you, honey?" She walked ahead of me into a sitting room. "Ruined my larynx, but I can't quit. I bum 'em from neighbors, and my granddaughter takes 'em away. Why the hell is it worth living? I always told George he'd survive me because he didn't smoke. But this is God's revenge. Been without my George for ten years now." She sounded like the voice of a computer from an old sci-fi movie.

I told her I didn't smoke, and she sighed, waving me to a dusty overstuffed sofa.

"I'm looking into a very old homicide case," I began.

"It's that girl," she said matter-of-factly. "Rebecca."

"What makes you say that?" I fell automatically into cop mode.

She blinked at me. "Well, it is, isn't it? That's why you're here."

"That's true, Mrs. Harvey. I'm just a little surprised you would know that."

"I have a better memory than anyone you'll ever meet, honey. Anyway, I knew they'd never let it rest."

I asked her what she meant.

She looked around the dim room and then looked back at me. "A lot of people thought it was the Creeper that got her," intoned the metallic monotone. I wanted to laugh, but a chill ran up the back of my neck.

"The what?"

"That's what they called him. "The Creeper." All that summer, he was out there. At first, the cops didn't want to believe it. Then when they couldn't solve Rebecca's killing, and the other killings happened, they didn't want to talk about it, because they never could catch him. My God, George bought a gun. We never left the doors unlocked after that summer."

She saw my expression, and her watery eyes brightened.

"My God, honey, didn't they tell you about him?"

"There was nothing in any of the reports—" I began.

"Oh hell," she interrupted. "When is anything important written down? They didn't want to write it down because they didn't want to believe it. And if the papers started writing about Jack the Ripper in the desert, it might hurt tourism and discourage all the people coming here from back east—that was George's theory. 'Keep Arizona green: Bring money.' "

"How did you know about this guy?"

"Everybody knew," she said, digging around the cushions of the sofa and finally coming up with a smoke. "People talked about it. Women alone at night talked about being followed. A woman over by Third and Cypress was attacked when she got out of her car one night. But her husband came out, and the Creeper ran."

It was about a block from my house.

She lit her cigarette, smiled angelically, and went on. "Another time, a woman woke up, and he was standing over her. For some reason, he didn't do anything. About a week after that, a girl was raped and beaten at Encanto Park. It went on all summer. Then poor Rebecca."

"Did you know her?"

"Oh, yes," Mrs. Harvey said, drawing hungrily on the cigarette. "I used to take her cookies on Sunday nights. She would run errands for me. She always seemed so alone. I mean, her uncle was the governor and all—they did tell you that, right?" I nodded. "But she seemed lonely. Not all that many girls were working then, and Rebecca seemed like such a sensitive soul. She loved poetry. Her favorite was T. S. Eliot, as I recall."

"How long before she disappeared did you see her?"

"We took her to the train, when she went back east. We wanted to pick her up, but I guess she didn't want to impose. She so wanted to be independent." Then she added, "To get away from that damned family of hers."

"You mentioned other killings?"

"He got a taste for it after Rebecca," said the mechanical voice. "Every eight or nine months, a girl would turn up in the desert. This went on, oh, another three years. The police never admitted they were connected, but we knew. And they never got him."

I asked her if people knew who the Creeper was.

"I always thought the cops knew who it was, but if you're here asking me, maybe they didn't. Who knows? That was when Phoenix changed. It wasn't a little town anymore. People were coming in from everywhere. Some stayed only a few years and moved on. There were the ones who came to work construction. There were the farmworkers. There were the snowbirds. Who knows?"

Phoenix is the newest and oldest of cities. The canals that carry its water past new skyscrapers and freeways are built on the waterworks of ancient Indians. When their civilization vanished, all that was left were their canals and the name a later tribe gave the canal builders: Hohokam, "the vanished ones." But the past is never past. We are living in their city. It is all connected.

The Hohokam came to the Salt River Valley about the same time Charlemagne was forging a new Europe out of the chaos of Rome's fall. In this isolated place, the Indians discovered one of the great fertile river valleys on earth. A thousand years later, a few Anglo settlers found it, too. They restored the Hohokam canals and built new ones. And with water, the Valley grew the vegetables and citrus and cotton that made families like the McConnicos wealthy. Everything is connected.

I hoped I had hold of a connection that might lead us to who had murdered Rebecca Stokes. It didn't seem like brain surgery. But I wasn't going to doubt my worth to Peralta right now. I needed that thousand-dollar fee. And God knows, I'd watched lots of my former colleagues in the ivory tower parlay the obvious into prestigious fellowships and acclaimed books. Anyway, I was intrigued by this murder. Some of the cases Peralta sent my way were as boring as an accounting exam. This one was different. This was a real mystery. I could almost feel the safe, cool desert night Rebecca stepped into from the train; feel the sinister chill that her disappearance cast over a small city.

Cops are conditioned to disbelieve almost everything they are told, but Opal Harvey's story was making more and more sense. I went back downtown, spent the afternoon reading old homicide records. Sure enough, there was a loose string of body dumps in the desert in the late 1950s and early 1960s that were never solved. Five young women, strangled and sexually assaulted, naked except for their bras, purses nearby with IDs and money, the killers never found. Two of the bodies were discovered east of town, near Superstition Mountain, and the others, including Rebecca, were found in the desolate Harquahala Desert, west of the White Tank Mountains. Most of the cases seemed to have languished in the Phoenix PD's Criminal Investigation Bureau under a detective named Harrison Wolfe, who disappeared in the early 1970s.

The idea of serial killers didn't enter the popular imagination until the late 1970s, but there were earlier examples of madmen who killed again and again such as the Boston Strangler. But there was nothing, on paper at least, that indicated the investigating officers were tying the cases together. And yet the victims were all young, single, middle-class working women with fair hair—two redheads and three blondes. I thought about what Opal Harvey had said about the city's powerful citizens being terrified that the killings would hurt economic growth. History was full of stranger motivations behind cover-ups.

The contents of the reports were only a start, though. I was beginning to realize how incomplete, and sometimes misleading, police reports could be. I spent Monday night and Tuesday morning trying to find other people involved in the Stokes case. Forty-plus years can erase a lot of lives. But I got another break when I tracked down a retired Phoenix cop whose name had appeared on the initial report of Rebecca's disappearance.

John Rogers was an enormous man, a Navajo, who was squeezed

into a wheelchair in the lobby of a middling nursing home on the west side. But his grip was very strong and his gaze very direct.

"You look too damned smart to be a deputy," he said. "When I was on the job, the Maricopa County Sheriff's Office was a joke. Bunch of fat boys running the jail."

I showed him my ID, but he waved it away.

"Hell, I'd see you even if you weren't a cop," he said. "First visit I've had in four years. My family, shit. My son's a lawyer in L.A., and my daughter's in detox somewhere. I guess they don't want to smell the shit and piss here. You married?"

I shook my head.

"You're lucky."

I told him why I was there, watching my story register in the ruin of cracks that encased his old eyes. A Phoenix cop to the end, he wanted to know why MCSO was investigating, and I reminded him that the bodies had been found in the county.

He closed his eyes for a moment and then said, "I took that missing person's report. From her uncle, the governor. He was a very worried man. The girl was supposed to have come home on the Golden State Limited the night before. She never went into work the next day."

I heard a woman's voice wailing off down a corridor.

"They found her about two weeks later," he went on, cocking his massive head. "A Public Service crew, as I remember it. Then they turned it over to the detectives, and that was that."

"If that was that, why do you remember it?"

"Oh, an old man's memory," he said. "She seemed so pretty, from her pictures. And back in those days, things like that hardly ever happened. It just stayed with me."

"Did you feel any pressure from the governor's office to keep the case quiet?"

"We were told by our sergeant not to say a word about it. The newspapers never said she was old man McConnico's niece."

I asked him if he remembered any other cases like it, and his face changed a bit, collapsed a little on itself.

"There were some others around that time."

"The Creeper?" I ventured.

"Whatever," John Rogers said. "I know that's what some cops were talking about. Shit, I was just a patrolman. Only Indian on the force. First Indian on the force."

I listed the other four body drops and asked why the detectives hadn't linked the cases.

"Who the hell knows?" he rasped, angry now. "Who knows why detectives do anything? No offense."

"None taken," I said. "Did you respond to any Creeper calls?"

"Not that I know of. But there were always prowlers, and some might have been him, if there was a Creeper. Nobody really knew."

"What did you think?"

He looked at me for a long moment. "What did I think? Let me tell you something. When that second girl was killed—Leslie was her name, I think—they found a Mexican who worked for the family gardener, and they thought they had their man. He'd been looking at her through the window at night; we knew that. Took him up to the fourth floor and beat him with saps for an hour, and he was ready to confess to anything. That's how it was done then. The dicks thought they had solved that one, so how could the cases be linked?"

"So why isn't that in the reports?"

"Because they beat him to death. Internal bleeding, didn't show up at first. He died in the city jail overnight. They put him in a pauper's grave, and that was that."

Tuesday night, I stayed home to write an update for Peralta. I also needed to go over my lecture notes for the American history survey I was teaching at Phoenix College—another few bucks for my dwindling bank account. And I wanted to rewire the back porch light. So I got comfort food—chilies rellenos from Ramiro's—settled behind Grandfather's old desk in the study off the living room, and booted up the PowerBook. That's when the doorbell rang.

Once again, Julie Riding was on my doorstep. This time, she wore a light blue denim shirt and blue jeans. Her hair was pulled back, and she looked startlingly like the Julie I had known twenty years before.

"I know I'm bothering you," she said. I said something polite and invited her in.

Back in the facing chairs, I told Julie what I had found out about her sister, which wasn't much. Her eyes were dreamy, unfocused, and she seemed drunk.

"I brought you something," she said, handing over an envelope. "It has some of Phaedra's things. Photos, an address book. That kind of thing."

In my mind, I was still back in the fifties—with young John Rogers and Opal Harvey and Rebecca Stokes—and the dissonance of being pulled back made me a little cross.

"Julie, I can't search for Phaedra," I said. "I'm barely making a living. I said I'd make some inquiries, and I did. No Jane Does who match her description in the postmortem lab. No body drops . . ."

When I looked up, Julie's face had reddened and she was crying. I instantly felt terrible.

"Sorry," I said. "I didn't mean to—"

"Goddamn you," she said, sniffling. "You are still angry with me after twenty years."

I poured us both a McClelland's. She lighted a smoke.

"Do you know what happened after I left you?" she said.

I made no response.

"I went to San Diego for a week with Chet, whom you were so threatened by. . . ."

"Yeah, he was a wealthy heart surgeon, and I was a college student and part-time deputy making ten thousand dollars a year," I said.

"And after a week, he told me he was going back to his wife. So I came back to Phoenix and started waiting tables."

"Why didn't you tell me?"

Julie ignored me. "You thought I had this great life because of my looks."

I started to protest, but she cut me off. "Yes, you did," she said. "But it wasn't a great life. I was so young, and I was just . . . just . . . overwhelmed by it all. All these men, all of them after me. I know you think it would be wonderful to be so desired, but it wasn't that way. You'll never know how lonely it is when somebody just wants to fuck you. I was just too young to know any better."

I don't know why I asked this, but it just came out: "Did you ever care about me?"

"Oh, David," she said in a voice I had heard so many times before. "That's history."

She drank the scotch. "I was so fucked up then. Nobody should have wanted me."

"I did," I ventured.

"You didn't know me," she said. Fair enough, I thought.

"We had a very unhappy home life," she went on. "I moved out when I was sixteen just to get away. I tried to keep you away from that. I was afraid if you knew, really knew about me, you'd just hate me."

"I would never have hated you. All those years, I wondered about you."

"Oh yeah," she said, her voice a mix of anger and irony. "Do you really want to know? All those years I spent in dead-end jobs, a pretty ornament on some guy's arm. I got into cocaine, and God, I loved it."

She stubbed out the cigarette and drank the last of her scotch. "There was always some asshole, thinking with his cock, who would buy it for me. Before he left me. Then I married a lawyer; God, what a mistake. He controlled me with coke and beat the shit out of me when I mouthed off to him. It was hell, but it was really hard to give up, too. Does that make any sense to you? I loved the money and the beautiful people and the feeling that the drugs gave me."

I walked to her chair, put my hand on her shoulder, and she came into my arms. I held her a long time while she cried silently, angrily.

"I'm a mess, David," she said finally. "Everything I touch turns bad."

CHAPTER 5

"She got the looks in the family," Julie said. "And the brains."

We had moved over to the sofa, where the pictures were spread between us. I used Kleenex and scotch to nurse Julie through the tears; then I put a Charlie Parker CD on low and we got to work. I knew she was mind-fucking me, but, hell, I was lonely and it was nice to be needed, if only for the moment and on unreliable terms.

The photos showed a young woman, pretty in a fair, red-haired way that stood out in Phoenix, with its battalions of tanned hotties. Her finely boned face had an intensely direct stare. Her smile had that ironic, mocking quality that reminded me of Julie long ago. And that hair: the natural shade of flame titian. Phaedra was beautiful in a way that would have been dangerous to me, but I was always a sucker for redheads.

Julie blew her nose and pulled out a pack of Marlboro Lights. "You're sure this is okay?"

"It was never a problem," I said, and she lighted it. "If I were more politically correct, I'd have tenure." I poured two more glasses of McClelland's and asked her to walk me through the past year of Phaedra's life.

"She'd been living with a man in Sedona. His name is Greg

Townsend. Twenty years older. His father made a fortune in real estate. Very well-off."

"Takes after her older sister?" I have such a mouth.

Julie smiled unhappily. "Anyway, they'd been living together for about three months."

"They met how?"

"Oh, who knows," Julie said. "She just told me she was in love, and that she was moving to Sedona."

"How did he treat her?"

"Oh, he took her to London, Paris. Mexico every other weekend, seemed like. He had his own airplane. Bought her clothes, Indian art, whatever she wanted, I guess. But who knows what he was really like. Some real bastards can spend lots of money on you."

"You two talked?"

"She'd call."

"Did she seem happy?"

"It was always hard to tell with Phaedra. At first, yes."

"Did he abuse her? Hurt her physically? Make threats?"

"No," Julie said, leaning forward, seeming to search for the words. "She never mentioned anything like that, although she had been in a relationship like that a few years ago. Greg was—I don't know, he seemed like a flake to me. New Age. One of these going-to-extremes athletes. Lots of money. But nothing real underneath."

"Well, you know what they say, 'No money, no life.' How'd it end?"

"Let me put it this way, David. Phaedra was always good at making her escape. I think she looked at Mom and Dad together, looked at all my disasters in love—God, what a bunch of role models!—and she decided she was never going to be trapped. Never going to be dependent on a man. She walked. Her relationships always had a short half-life. Greg was no different. Phaedra called me one Sunday and said she was back in Phoenix, asked if she could stay with me a few days."

"That was when?"

"In the spring. April, I guess."

Julie said her sister got a job as an assistant to a photographer who had done some work for the Phoenician. I jotted the photographer's name below Greg Townsend's on the envelope. Phaedra started seeing a therapist and attending family gatherings again. She found a one-bedroom apartment in Scottsdale. She and Julie talked on the phone almost every night.

"Did she meet anybody else?"

"Nobody serious," Julie said.

"Flirtations? One-night stands?"

Julie shrugged like an older sister. "She was fairly burned out on relationships. She felt very suffocated by Greg."

"And nothing struck you as strange in the days or weeks before her disappearance? Nobody new in her life? Nothing about her personality that changed? No sense she felt in danger?"

"No. She seemed to be very healthy about it all. Which was new for Phaedra, because when she'd break up with a lover, she would usually just fall apart for a while. I was very distracted, though. My ex and I were in court. Visitation, custody, all that. Work was a nightmare."

We talked maybe another half hour. Then I walked her out to her car, just like the other night.

The sun was gone, and the street was deserted except for a few parked cars. I could hear a set of sirens over on Seventh Avenue, running north from downtown.

"I'm not trying to be a selfish bitch," Julie said. "I just need help. Phaedra is the only family I have really. Dad died five years ago, and Mom is more and more out of it. I just feel so scared about Phaedra."

"I understand," I said, and realized I had stepped into something that could have a really bad ending. I pushed the thought away.

We hugged out in the ovenlike heat, and for just a moment, stroking her hair, I felt like I had twenty years ago. Then she kissed me on the mouth, a nice kiss, and she drove away.

Back inside, Charlie Parker had finished and the house felt as if it hadn't been lived in for a hundred years. I looked around, freshly aware of how odd or brilliant Grandfather's floor plan was. The high-ceiling living room with bookcases behind a stairway that went nowhere—well, it went to the garage apartment in back, via an open-air passage. The illusion of space, when the house only had two small bedrooms. The quirky charm of a garden courtyard off the little study that connected to the living room. I suddenly missed my grandparents so much. Wished I could walk into the dining room and find Grandmother watching her soap operas. Wished I could get a whiff of Grandfather's pipe as he paced in his study. Even Patty had loved this house—she'd encouraged me to rent it out after my grandparents died, rather than sell. At times like this, I didn't know if I could bear to part with it, or if I could bear another night in it.

It was not a good mind-set in which to receive a full-mouth French kiss from an old girlfriend. I poured another scotch, wished it wasn't too hot to sit in the garden, ended up on the staircase, absently perusing the books that Grandfather, and then I, had stacked onto the old shelves.

Julie Riding was not the great love of my life. But she was my first real girlfriend. "Real" in the sense that I lost my virginity to her, at the shameful old age of nineteen. "Real" in that we stayed together, more or less, for two years and sometimes I felt like I loved her.

We built the kinds of traditions that twenty-year-olds build. I was very proud to have her on my arm. I think she thought I was "smart," but what did that mean to a young woman like Julie? I remember she never liked books. And I wasn't at all like the rock-star clones she seemed to moon over.

Did we love each other? Who knows? Who knows anything at that age. Who knows anything now? The heart is such a mystery.

I do remember the first time I saw her, walking away from me on the mall at ASU, all blond straight hair and long legs and youth. We would never know less sadness in our lives than that first time we stayed out all night talking, then spent the morning in each other's arms in the safe chill of the air-conditioned darkness. Every possibility that life held was open to us. And every mistake.

I dreamed about Julie that night, dreaming in the heavy sleep that comes after a day spent in the desert heat. But whatever we said and did was forgotten in the sudden smashing of bumpers and screeching of tires out on the street. I was immediately awake. The clock read 3:30.

My bedroom fronts the street. I could hear shouts and cursing in English and Spanish. Then threats. Then a gunshot, sharp and deep. Then another two—higher-pitched, maybe a .22.

I dropped painfully to the floor, grabbed up the cordless phone, and dialed 911. Talking to the dispatcher, I crawled over to the window and cautiously lifted one blind. They were gone, not a body left behind, not a trace. Just the vivid white circle of the streetlight. Four minutes had passed. I explained three times to the 911 operator that I hadn't seen the incident, only heard it. I told her it wasn't necessary for an officer to make contact.

When I was growing up in this neighborhood, even in the turmoil of the 1960s, it had seemed the safest place in the world. The biggest worry for parents was the traffic on Seventh Avenue. Now there were no safe places. I pulled on some shorts, went into the garage, and pulled a dusty, slender box out of a carton I had brought back from San Diego, along with my books and lecture notes. Inside was a Colt Python .357 with a four-inch barrel and ammunition. When I was a deputy, this had been my pride and joy—"one of the finest handguns in the world," Peralta had pronounced—and had cost about a month's worth of paychecks. It had less usefulness for a college professor. I hadn't seen the revolver for a month, since I qualified at the range to get my deputy credentials and keep Peralta off my back. I took the box back inside, turned out the light, and listened a long time in the darkness until sleep came again.

Phaedra Riding's apartment sat fifty feet back from Hayden Road in south Scottsdale, on the second floor of one of the cookie-cutter stucco complexes that popped up around the city back in the 1970s. The front door faced a courtyard, with its pool, landscaping, and ornamental lights, while a rear balcony looked out on a parking lot and, beyond a stand of olive trees, the street. This part of Scottsdale lacked the moneyed glitz of the resorts and walled-off neighborhoods a few miles farther north, but it was still comfortable and pleasant. I used the key Julie had given me to let myself in.

The place was gently disheveled, clothes and books strewn about, and it had that expectant smell of pricey perfumes and broken-in denim that you find in the apartments of some young women. A pile of old mail was on the desk—nothing but some bills and advertisements. The room was dominated by a watercolor from a Santa Fe artist. Several gorgeous pieces of Acoma and Santa Clara pottery sat under a light sheen of dust on a shelf. In one corner was a music stand, chair and a cello case. Monochromatic Scandinavian furniture: tasteful, minimalist, and expensive. Not exactly like my apartment when I was twenty-eight—or now.

Back in the bedroom, a queen-sized bed was neatly made. More clothes were piled onto a wicker basket. She had photos of Julie and her parents on the bedside table, as well as a paperback copy of *Atlas Shrugged*. I whispered the book's first line in my head: "Who is John Galt?" I picked carefully through drawers, looked under her bed, pulled up the mattress. The closet was full of clothes and two pieces of luggage, both empty. The bathroom was spotless, but if she was off with a new lover, as Peralta was so sure, she'd left her diaphragm and a partly used tube of spermacide in the medicine chest.

I closed the cabinet gently enough to hear a movement on the carpet behind me, then to see a shadow against the wall. I'd like to say I didn't jump.

"No, you get back," she yelled, holding out a small can of Mace.

"Wait, I'm a cop," I said, the words sounding so strange to me. She stepped back to the bedroom door. "I'm going to reach in my pocket for an ID." I opened up the wallet with my star and identification. She read it, compared my face with the one on the ID card, and reluctantly put the Mace down.

She was not Phaedra, but she looked the way I might imagine Phaedra in, say, fifteen years. She was slim and fairly tall, wore a tailored charcoal gray suit, its skirt cut above the knees. Her strawberry blond hair fell to just above her shoulders, and her fine, high cheekbones had a heavy dusting of freckles. She stood, wary, watching me with green eyes.

"Mapstone," she said. "What kind of name is that?"

"Welsh."

"Ah. You look more like a college professor than a deputy," she said. "What are you doing here?"

"I might ask you the same thing," I said. "And I will. But I'd like to know who you are."

"I'm Phaedra's boss," she said. "Susan Knightly. I run the photo studio where Phaedra was working. She's my assistant."

She dug into her shoulder bag and handed me a business card:

"Something's wrong, isn't it?" Susan Knightly asked.

"I don't know," I said. "Phaedra's sister filed a missing person's report."

"Julie," she said, with something untranslatable in those green eyes. "I know about that. Have you found her?"

I shook my head.

"I've been watering her plants, keeping an eye on the place. Phaedra had given me a key."

That struck me as odd. Why hadn't Julie told me this?

"Do you know where Phaedra is?" I asked.

"No idea," she said. "She told me she might need to take a few days to take care of some business, and she asked me if I'd water her plants. Then I didn't hear a word from her. I've been worried, but I didn't know what else to do but wait, since Julie went to the police and all."

"That's how she put it? 'Take care of some business'?" She nodded. "Did Phaedra seem different, upset?"

"She was a creative person, very tightly wound. But, yeah, she seemed, you know, strung out about something."

"But no idea what?"

"No," she said. "Here, help me water." We went to the kitchen and filled a couple of pitchers. "Give the cactus just a shot. Give the ivies lots of water."

"What kind of an employee was she?" I asked, moving over to one shelf of greenery.

"Very conscientious. Very hardworking. Being a photographer's assistant can be real shit work, pardon my French. But Phaedra really worked."

I asked Susan Knightly about her photo business.

"You have to do a little of everything to survive in this town. Some PR, some freelance for *Phoenix Magazine,* advertising, social scene. I don't do weddings and babies, if that's what you mean." She examined me to see if I was a philistine, but declined to share the verdict. "I had a show at the Gilbert Gallery in Scottsdale earlier this year."

I nodded, then asked, "Do you have any reason to believe Phaedra might have been a victim of foul play?"

"Of course I do," she said, her voice gathering intensity. "That's such a stupid cop question. Look at the newspaper every day: drive-by shootings, kidnappings and rapes, random killings. My neighbor was mugged a week ago in broad daylight. An attractive young woman just doesn't disappear like this."

"My boss thinks she's off with a new boyfriend. She has a history of that, you know."

"Tell your boss I think he's a pig," she said. Then her face softened. "Phaedra really wants to be a photographer. It really bit her, and she's worked hard. Has a good eye, too. Tell me why she would just walk away from the chance I was giving her, no matter how sexy a new boyfriend might be?"

It was a good question, and I didn't have an answer for it yet.

I left Susan Knightly to finish watering the plants while I knocked on doors. I had deliberately come early to find people at home, but the neighbors had only a passing knowledge of Phaedra. Such was the norm in a transient city.

"She's sure loud when she has sex," the woman next door told me, blushing. "Makes me envious." But the woman didn't even know Phaedra's name, much less actually see any men or realize she'd been gone for weeks. "I thought it was pretty quiet lately," she allowed. The landlord said Ms. Riding had paid her rent three months ahead, and that was really all he cared about. By the time I left, I had again become accustomed to flashing my badge to get people to talk to me.

I had to move on. Class was at 10:30, but it went by quickly: lecture and discussion on the origins of the Civil War, two chapters to read before Friday. By the time I drove the three miles from Phoenix College to the Sheriff's Office downtown, the temperature was well over 110 degrees. I regretted that I had worn a blue shirt, and I ran the Blazer's air-conditioning on high to make some of the sweat disappear.

I spent the afternoon in Central Records, working on the Stokes case. If Rebecca Stokes had run into a serial killer nicknamed "the Creeper," who was he and what might have happened to him?

I'm not great with computers, but a young deputy named Lindsey showed me how I could set up search parameters to comb the database for certain kinds of offenders from that era.

Lindsey had straight black hair, pale skin, a small gold stud in her left nostril, and very shapely legs set off by sheer black panty hose and a black miniskirt. She was pretty, but with a look of constant sardonic detachment. She asked why I wasn't smiling, and I said, "I'm smiling inside." She adjusted her oval tortoiseshell glasses and said, "There are no ironic deputies." Then she smirked at me, and we became fast friends.

We looked for men with convictions for murder, assault, or rape, along with ones convicted of breaking and entering, who might have been in Phoenix in the late 1950s. We checked files from MCSO, the Phoenix Police Department, the Arizona Department of Corrections, and NCIC, the National Crime Information Center. By four o'clock, we had built a program to look for what we wanted. While Lindsey ran the computer, I looked the old-fashioned way, through my cache of records over at the old courthouse and in the microfilm of old newspapers. All this was an imprecise exercise, dealing with old data and a hundred variables, but it was information Peralta would want.

Wednesday night, I had dinner by myself at a little Cuban place off Camelback Road. I read Lindsey's report and sipped a Negra Modelo from the bottle. Then, full and comfortable, I went back into the heat and drove home.

I turned onto my street just as the digital clock on the Blazer's dash turned a phosphorescent green 10:00. The houses nearby were dark, the only sign of life being the sound of wind chimes across the street. When I was growing up, we all knew our neighbors. On the west was Mrs. Street, a widow who gave chocolate-chip cookies to the neighborhood kids. On the east were the Calhouns—I'd had a mammoth crush on Kathy Calhoun. Across the street were the Jarvises and the Herolds and old man Goodman—he hated it when we kids made noise. They were all gone now. I couldn't tell you who my neighbors were. For ten years after my grandmother's death, I had rented the house, returning only rarely. That seemed to have been enough time for the block to become a stranger to me.

Into the carport, out into the heat. I was in that happy, sleepy state after a good dinner, and looking forward to reading Iris Chang's book, *The Rape of Nanking*—I was about halfway through it, and it was riveting, moving; a stunning work. Not the kind of impenetrable mess history professors are encouraged to write nowadays. Oh well. I could always work for Mike Peralta. I closed up the Blazer and walked toward the back door.

He must have been hiding in the oleander to the east of the carport, because I never saw him. I only felt it when he hit me hard on the back of the neck. My knees just gave out and I instantly wanted to throw up. I didn't even think of fighting back. For what seemed like several minutes, I couldn't even feel my arms and legs.

"I could kill you right here, hero," he hissed in my ear, and I felt a gun barrel, surprisingly cold, considering the hot night, press against the side of my face. I was beyond coherent thoughts. I was scared as hell. "Some fucking cop you are." He had very bad breath. "You're in way over your head." A sharp kick in my side. "The message is: 'Back away.' Back away. Get the message, or I can find you again."

That was all I heard before I passed out.

The first time I ate a plate of Sharon Peralta's trademark chicken enchiladas was fifteen years ago. I had worked my last shift as a deputy sheriff; I was a freshly minted Ph.D. in history, with a new job at a midwestern college; I was anticipating living away from hot, dry Phoenix for the first time in my life, and I ate way too much. Now, Friday night, I was still hurting from the ignominious ass-kicking of two nights before, and our conversation about life, work, and Phoenix was nonstop. But I still managed to polish off four of those wonderful enchiladas. I helped clear the table while Sharon and Mike fussed; then Mike steered me into the study for cigars and cognac.

The Peraltas had an airy new house in far north Phoenix, situated just below some of the low, bare mountains that once sat nameless and secluded well outside the city limits. While most of the house reflected Sharon's careful touch, the study was cluttered with western furniture, a couple of knockoff Remington sculptures, three walls of books, more photos and awards, and a very large oak gun cabinet. This was Mike's room. He went to his humidor, extracted two large dark brown cigars, and gave me one.

"Anniversario Padron," he said, cutting it for me. "Make sure you light it evenly. Let the smoke waft across your palate."

Sharon, wearing blue jeans and a white cotton short-sleeved blouse, her long black hair pulled over one shoulder, sat opposite us with a glass of white wine. "If I haven't left him over this cigar habit, I guess we're together for life," she said, wrinkling her nose.

"You know you love this, honey," Mike Peralta said, puffing and rolling the cigar as he lit it.

"I think it has interesting Freudian undertones," she said, sniffing.

Mike and Sharon had been childhood sweethearts. By the time I met Mike, they had been married nearly five years. Now they had two grown kids and managed to make a good life for themselves. God knows, it couldn't have been easy living with Mike, and I knew they came close to breaking up while Mike and I were partners years ago—but somehow they had made it.

If Mike had barely changed, Sharon had become nearly unrecognizable from the person I knew fifteen years ago. Then, she was a pudgy, shy social worker who was fighting her husband about continuing her schooling. I guess she won, because she went on to get her doctorate in psychology, go into private practice, write a popular book on eating disorders, and, for the past two years, host a radio psychologist show on a local station. Dr. Sharon was a minor celebrity now, poised, polished, and aerobicized. Another thing that struck me was how Sharon had a calming influence on Mike. His coiled anger seemed subdued that night, his mood almost playful.

I sat back on the brown leather sofa, dragged on the cigar, and felt peaceful. My ribs still hurt like hell, though. I hadn't told Peralta about the encounter in the carport. I couldn't say exactly why. I guess I felt stupid for being so careless. Not only was Peralta a kind of big-brother figure to me, but he was my old self-defense instructor. I couldn't bear to admit to him that I had been on the losing end of a fight.

I'd come to in the carport maybe half an hour after I'd passed out, with a big tomcat licking my face and purring at me. I was covered in sweat and my head felt like I had been through a week-long binge of drinking bad whiskey. I pulled myself into the house, locked up behind me, and thought about what had happened and why. I wasn't as scared as I was surprised, and then angry, and then embarrassed. Working the streets for four years as a patrol deputy, I had seen plenty of violent situations, especially the family fights where the cops are target number one, and I had learned to take care of myself. But it was clear that years of the soft, safe life of academia had settled into me far more than I wanted to admit.

As to the why: I didn't have a clue. I couldn't imagine my work on the Stokes case mattering to anyone. I doubted it was some Marxist historian trying to settle an intellectual score with me; they had gotten me kicked off the faculty already. So it had to involve Phaedra. I hadn't been prepared to draw a conclusion Wednesday night, and I still wasn't. I'd called Julie Riding the next morning to see if she was okay, but she was distracted with work and we didn't talk long. I didn't tell her about the attack, either.

"So when are you going to bring me Stokes, signed, sealed, and delivered?" Peralta asked.

"Soon," I said. "Tell me why you tossed this case my way?"

"No," Sharon interjected. "No more work talk. I am sick to death of work talk."

"You do shrink talk," Peralta protested through a plume of cigar smoke.

"Not tonight, my love," she said. "We're going to talk about David."

I shifted uncomfortably and nursed the cognac.

"Mike tells me Julie Riding has come back into your life," Sharon said. I nodded and told her about the search for Phaedra.

"What's Julie like now? What's she doing?"

"Everybody changes," I said. "She's not the same woman I knew twenty years ago."

"I bet she's gotten old and ugly," Peralta said.

"You are so low," Sharon said, then turned back to me. "I don't know if I should say this. I never thought Julie was right for you, David. Too immature, too insecure. You two were so different. You gave a lot more than you got."

"That was a long time ago, Sharon. I have no illusions about Julie. I just told her I'd help her find her little sister, Phaedra."

"That's a pretty name," Sharon said.

"Ahhh." Mike puffed. "She's just run off with some boyfriend, or to get a tattoo or some Doc Martens, or whatever the hell it is they do now. Probably has a ring in her nose."

"Not from the pictures I saw," I said.

"And where has Phaedra gone?" Sharon asked.

I shrugged my shoulders.

"Are you sure she hasn't killed herself?"

I shook my head.

"Young women can get into a lot of trouble at that age," she said.

"Sharon thinks you need somebody in your life," Peralta said.

"Mike!" she said. Then: "Are you seeing anyone?"

I shook my head. "I've only been back in town a couple of months. I'm not really looking."

"Not carrying a torch for Patty?"

"No," I said a little too emphatically. "She's been through several lovers since me. Now she's with a twenty-two-year-old tennis pro."

"Well, none of my business," Sharon said. "You need some time. Everybody does after what you've been through. But you're very different from most people, David. I can't help my matchmaker impulses."

"Thanks, Sharon."

"And we both hope you'll stay in Phoenix. This is your home. This is where your roots and friends are, and as we get older, those things get more important."

I believed that, but my relationship with Phoenix was complicated. Being back in town seemed like the most natural thing in the world. There were new freeways and neighborhoods. The water-conservation policies had converted many lawns to desert landscaping. But it was still my city. Camelback and Squaw Peak and the South Mountains again became my dramatic compass as I drove the predictable grid of streets. The nights had the old familiar quality of dry, open spaces. I felt safe and centered here—a feeling that surprised me, given how burned-out I'd been when I left Phoenix years ago.

But the city had also become so big and dangerous. There was the heat and lack of rain, which I would always hate. And there was the job situation. Despite being an alumnus, I didn't receive a warm homecoming from Arizona State University, which said in a curt letter that it had a hiring freeze on, and even if it hadn't, my published articles as a historian had been "lackluster" and all hiring had to be done under the goal of "greater diversity." I only hoped I could find a new job before my savings ran out.

"But for now, he needs work," Peralta said, reading my mind. "So what did the cops forty years ago miss about Rebecca Stokes?"

Sharon started to object to work talk, but she stopped when I said, "They missed a serial killer."

Peralta sat silently, wreathed in bluish cigar smoke, letting me lay it all out. I told them about Opal Harvey, the Creeper, John Rodgers. One by one, I detailed the four other homicides of young women and their similarity to the Stokes case. Sharon's large coffee-colored eyes never left me.

Finally, after a long silence, Peralta let out a huge sigh and said, "Jesus."

He refilled our glasses with cognac. "It's not airtight that these are related, but it's pretty compelling. Especially for the little town Phoenix was in those days. I'd never heard of any of these other cases."

"I didn't find any newspaper accounts of the others," I said. "But they probably didn't have Rebecca's family connections."

Peralta asked, "How come the cops back then didn't make this connection?"

"That's the big question," I said. "The lead detective on Stokes was a man named Harrison Wolfe, and I can't find him, can't even find a record of his death. He might know. Opal Harvey thought the powers that be didn't want to attract the negative publicity."

"Never underestimate the amount of ass-covering cops can do," Peralta said. "Harrison Wolfe. I've heard of him. He was very old school. When I went to the Academy, there were still stories about Harrison Wolfe."

"Such as?" Sharon asked.

"Oh, racist, sexist, politically incorrect stuff, honey." Peralta smiled.

"So you like him," Sharon teased.

Peralta went on. "He was a hard-ass. There was a story that was still making the rounds when I was a rookie in the early seventies about how years before this cop came on some bad guys down at the Southern Pacific yards one night, caught them breaking into a boxcar, but they had him surrounded and had their guns on him. The son of a bitch pulled his own gun—drew against the drop—and killed two of them, wounded the two others. His name was Harrison Wolfe."

"Sounds like a whackadoo to me," she said. "Clinically speaking, of course."

"So what else have you found?" Peralta asked.

"There was some newspaper coverage of Rebecca's disappearance, but there was not a word—that I could find, anyway—to indicate she was the governor's niece. But everybody seemed to know it anyway. That small-town thing again."

"Suspects?"

"I'm working with Records to pull up a list of likelies for you: Felony convictions involving breaking and entering, assault, rape and/or murder in the Southwest during those approximate years."

"But the killings just stopped?" Sharon asked.

"As far as I can tell," I said. "In 1962, a flight attendant named Gloria Johnson disappeared, then turned up a few days later under the same circumstances. Then nothing, at least for the next several years."

"Sometimes they just stop," Peralta said. "Green River stopped, or died or was killed, or maybe arrested for something else. Serial killers aren't nearly as neat and methodical as in the movies. And there are more unsolved murders than the cops would ever like to admit." He thought for a moment and then said, "I wish this Harquahala bastard would die."

* * *

I drove home in a contented buzz through light late-night traffic on Squaw Peak Parkway. But I had retrieved my old holster for the .357 Python and now both sat ominously in the Blazer's glove compartment. I wasn't ready to start packing all the time—it was hard to conceal a weapon in this heat—but I wanted it nearby. I kept wondering who wanted me to back off investigating Phaedra's disappearance. And why. One thing that was clear now was that Julie's apprehensions were correct. Her little sister was into something bad.

At home an hour later, I was on-line, plugged into MCSO Central Records and running Phaedra and her old boyfriends through the National Crime Information Center, when there was a knock at the office door. I jumped at the sound. Then I unholstered the heavy revolver and stepped to the side of the door to look out. Too dark. Damn burned-out light.

"Who's there?" I said. It was 2:13 A.M.

"Julie. It's Julie."

I set the pistol on a table and opened the door.

Julie Riding stepped in quickly and wrapped her arms around me. She was trembling. I closed the door and locked it.

"I'm really scared," she said, and for a long time, she stayed in my arms, shaking from time to time as if she was cold. I watched my unattended PowerBook put itself to sleep, and the only light in the room was Grandfather's green-shaded banker's lamp, which had fascinated me when I was a little boy.

"What is it, Julie?"

"I really need a drink, David."

I steered her over to the leather couch and poured us both scotch. Julie had changed her hair again. It was straighter, parted at the center, and closer to her natural shade of light brown/blond. Her eyes glistened. When I sat next to her, she said, "I think someone is following me."

My eyes automatically sought out the reassurance of the Python on the table.

"Did someone follow you here tonight?"

She shook her head. "I took a really roundabout route."

"Where's your daughter?"

"With her dad. We have joint custody, and Mindy's with him all month." She sighed. "That's not true. He has custody. She sees me every other weekend. Don't ask, David. That's what happens when you get in a court battle with a fucking lawyer." She pushed her hair back.

I asked her why she thought someone was following her.

"I noticed him when I came here the other night. A man sitting in a black Mustang convertible. It's strange enough to see somebody sitting in a car on a residential street late at night. Something about him really gave me the creeps, but I put it out of my mind, you know? Then I saw him again when I left work yesterday. He was just sitting in the parking lot for hotel employees. Tonight, I went out with some girlfriends, and afterward, when I was walking to my car, I turned around and he was walking behind me, maybe half a block back. Just walking behind me. He was small, but really muscled up. And when I pulled out, that black Mustang was right behind me." She swallowed her drink. "I lost him on the freeway."

"How do you know the man in the parking lot was the same man who was sitting out here the other night?"

"It was him," Julie said. "He had scary eyes. The first time I saw him in the car, I was so curious that I looked in at him, and he looked right back at me. And he had on a leather jacket both times I saw him. Lots of shiny silver zippers."

"In this heat?"

"Yes," she said.

"Julie, was Phaedra into anything you haven't told me about?"

"No," she said. "You think this is about Phaedra?"

"I don't know. The other night somebody put a gun to my head and told me to back off. He didn't mention Phaedra, but I can't imagine he meant a forty-year-old case I'm working on for Peralta. And he was waiting for me when I got home, so obviously he knew where I lived."

Julie was silent for several minutes, sitting on the couch with her legs tucked underneath her. I refilled her glass and sipped at mine. I was listening to the house and the street, but everything sounded normal. Then I heard the sound of Julie holding back sobs. I put my hand on hers, and she leaned over to me and hugged me tightly.

"I've made so many mistakes with my life," she cried, digging her nails into me. "I can't bear to lose her, too. You've got to help me find her."

"I am, Julie. I will."

She cupped my face in her hands and started kissing me. It was not a bad feeling. In fact, it was a damned nice feeling. Her mouth was warm and wet. Her tongue darted in my mouth.

"Baby, help me. Help your Julie," she whispered in between kisses. That was the way she had said things of great urgency and intimacy years before, punctuated by "your Julie."

"It's okay." I reluctantly turned my face away. "I'm going to find her."

Julie was pressed full against me now, both of us sideways on the sofa. I felt her nipples harden under the thin fabric of her blouse. I was tired and a little tight and not thinking clearly. When she turned her face expectantly up to mine again, I kissed her hungrily and our mouths and our hands spent a long time getting to know each other again.

Oscar Wilde said the only thing to do with history is to rewrite it, and I suppose that's what we might have done that night. I might have rewritten our lives together—as if that first brave flush of love could somehow have been sheltered long enough from the world and our own restless personalities to take root and grow. So that the young woman who was Julie twenty years before had given me her wondrous youth and beauty, free of the damage of the years, had given me her body and spirit and our children. And I would have given her in return everything I had to give. Julie was trying to rewrite a history known only to her. Maybe it was a history that allowed her peace from her private demons. Maybe it found Phaedra alive and safe. Maybe it was a happy ending for all of us.

I was starting to recall Julie's lovemaking with delicious clarity—the way she would always arch her back just a bit, the way she would take my face in her hands as she kissed me—when something made me stop. I gently pushed away from her on the couch.

"I can't do this yet," I said. She looked flushed and angry.

I don't know why I didn't take her to bed that night. The search for Phaedra wasn't a real investigation yet, just an old friend making some checks. So it wasn't an ethical problem, really, especially since I hadn't slept with a woman for more months than I cared to admit. But something in Julie, or something in me, made me pull back.

"I have to go now," she said, and wheeled around and ran out the door.

Time does strange things in the Arizona summer. It was late July now, and the only reality was the sun. Two weeks had passed, but I knew it only from scanning the date on each morning's newspaper. Otherwise, time had become meaningless in the yearly struggle of Phoenicians against the heat. Maybe a year had gone by. Maybe a day.

This was the mean season, when the weather seemed to bring out the worst in everybody. Day after day of 110 degrees or better left people exhausted, impatient, and sometimes violent. The newspaper seemed to carry more three-paragraph briefs about murders. A new mother battering her crying baby's head against the refrigerator only made it to the local section. The front page told about power outages on the fringes of the city, leaving thousands of people without air conditioning. Another story warned of an increase in greens fees for golfers. The price for living in paradise.

I spent most of my time tying up loose ends on the Stokes case, and I felt pretty good about it. Lindsey Adams, my new pal in Records, had come up with a list of seventeen likely suspects that met our search parameters. She was the master of databases. Her fingers flew across the computer keyboard as her delicate mouth, dark with a black-red lipstick, pursed in thought. Her tossed-off comments—

"he was wetting his noodle" being a favorite—made this more fun than most research.

As we listened to Lindsey's collection of seventies music—a strange hobby, she admitted—we looked at the potential suspects in detail, narrowing our list to four. They were bad men: killers, rapists, predators from a time that we forget had predators. Each was in the safe, small Valley of the Sun when Rebecca Stokes disappeared. One in particular had gotten out of the Arizona State Prison just three months before her murder; he had been serving a sentence for assaulting a woman outside her home in Tucson. And he ended up in the Valley: Prison records showed he had taken a job on parole, working as a laborer. The same man, Eddie Evans, died in a knife fight down in the Deuce five years later—a couple of years after the last of the unsolved murders of young women.

I delivered it all to Peralta in a report complete with photos, color graphics, and maps. It wouldn't hold up in court, but it didn't have to. All of the potential suspects were dead, as were the local bigs who hadn't wanted publicity about the unsolved murders of young women. Whatever embarrassment the case might once have caused was long past. But we knew more now about the murders of five human beings, and who might have been behind them. And that meant a thousand dollars to me from the county. It wasn't exactly history, and it wasn't exactly police work. "It's consulting," Lindsey, the postmodern woman, said.

Peralta called a 9:00 A.M. press conference to announce that the Sheriff's Office had new information on a notorious forty-year-old murder case. He was in his element with the lights and cameras, wearing his crisply pressed dress uniform with the three stars on the collars, and his badge, which was polished to a high shine.

It was a remarkable piece of theater, with slides, charts, and press kits for the reporters. A TV crew from *Unsolved Mysteries* flew in to be there. Frankly, I was surprised the sheriff let him do it alone—given the sheriff's penchant for hogging the media spotlight. But I didn't really know the tensions or alliances that marked the sheriff's relationship with his chief deputy. Peralta introduced me, and the next morning I found myself on the *Republic*'s front page, in a sidebar headlined HISTORY PROFESSOR CRACKS OLD CASES. That made me a little uncomfortable, since we hadn't exactly "cracked" a case. And I remember catching the date of the newspaper: July 23—it had been exactly a month since Phaedra had disappeared. But these were momentary misgivings. Lindsey even sent me a *Disco Inferno* CD as a reminder of how listening to it had inspired us, or so she said. All in all, I was feeling good about myself. Too good.

A little before noon on Friday, the phone rang.

"Deputy Mapstone?"

It was a fine, radio-quality voice.

"This is Brent McConnico. I was wondering if I could buy you lunch and thank you for the work you did on my cousin's case?"

I was a little taken aback. I had seen Brent McConnico's classically handsome face on TV many times since I'd gotten back to town. He was the young majority leader of the state senate, a favorite of Republican politicos and the scion of one of the state's oldest political families. But I had never met him or spoken to him before.

"Well, you don't owe me any thanks, Mr. McConnico," I said.

"Oh, please call me Brent," he said. "My father was Mr. McConnico." Without even a pause, he went on. "How about the Pointe at Tapatio Cliffs? Really stunning view of the city. Say Monday?"

"Sure," I said. "Brent."

I hung up and called Julie at work, but her voice mail answered and I hung up. I hadn't talked to her since the night we ended up in each other's arms. I didn't know what to say to her about us, if there was an "us." And I didn't have anything fresh to report about Phaedra. No young woman. No blue Nissan Sentra. Neither the computer nor phone calls to the numbers in her address book had yielded any information. I was stuck.

The Pointe at Tapatio Cliffs is a resort hotel perched in the Phoenix Mountain Preserve in the north part of the city. I walked past the spotless tennis courts, deserted in the midday heat, and made my way into the main restaurant and the blessed air-conditioning. I was wearing my best suit, navy blue with a thin pinstripe, and a

Frank Sinatra tie that had been Patty's last Christmas gift to me. I looked good, but this wasn't the weather for suits. I sat for twenty minutes in the dim coolness near the hostess's stand before Brent McConnico strode briskly in, spotted me, and held out his hand.

"You're taller than you seemed on TV," he said.

He had a firm grip, and his light blue eyes gazed at me with an easy directness. "Well, anybody would look smaller compared to Mike Peralta," I said.

"Yes, dear Mike," he said. "He'll probably be governor someday."

McConnico was shorter than I, maybe a little under six feet. But he obviously worked out, his body neatly turned out in a gray sack suit. He had politicians' hair, perfectly blow-dried. Light brown, it fell just over his ears. He turned me toward the restaurant, where the breathtakingly beautiful blond hostess greeted him by name and breezily led us to "his usual" table. He ordered a club soda. I ordered a Bombay Sapphire martini. Before us, as promised, was a stunning view of the city, looking toward downtown and the South Mountains.

"When our families first came to the Valley, all this was farmland, David," he said. "It just amazes me every day how much it's changed. How much it's changed even from when I was a boy."

I agreed with him. He'd obviously done a little homework to say that "our families" had been among the pioneers. It's natural in Phoenix to assume that everyone is from somewhere else. The joke says if you're here for five years, you're a native.

"But I know you can tell me much more history than I can tell you." He smiled. "You went to ASU?"

"I think one semester I had more parking tickets than any student in school history."

He laughed out loud. "Well, it's a fine school. I wanted to go there, but my mother insisted that I go back east. Yale. Then Harvard Law. I hated it at first. It all seemed so phony."

"School matters," I said. "I wish I had gone back east."

"It only matters so far," Brent McConnico said. "Tell me how in the world you went from law enforcement to academia, and now I guess you're back in police work again."

I gave him the short version. Years of teaching had given me a good sense of how much to say before people got bored.

"I think my dad knew your family," he said. "Your grandfather was his dentist for a while, before he retired. I remember he used to have his office just off Central, down by the Heard Museum."

"Arizona's a small world, even now," I said. He hadn't exactly put me at ease, but he didn't seem like a total silver spoon, either. I found myself liking him.

"As I said on the phone, I wanted to thank you for what you did to help us understand what might have happened to Rebecca," he said. "There have been a lot of questions all these years."

"Did you know her?"

"I don't have much memory of her," he said. "I was about six when she disappeared. She was kind to me. What I mainly remember is how it changed things for our family. For about a year, Mother wouldn't let me or my sisters play outside in the yard. I don't think there was any danger, but Rebecca's killing was . . . well, nothing was ever the same for us. That violence was always with us.

"As for Rebecca, I remember she liked to sit with me and help me play with my little trucks." He smiled slightly and shook his head. "That made her seem okay to me. But I didn't really understand what had happened when she disappeared and was murdered. We children weren't told much. And Mother and Dad never really wanted to talk about it. They felt guilty, I think. She had come here from her family in Chicago, and Dad wanted to look out for her, help her where he could. He and his brother, my uncle James, weren't especially close. But Dad really cared about Rebecca, I think, as if she had been his daughter rather than his niece. He got her the job at Larkin, Reading and Page."

"The law firm, right?"

"Yes, she was Sam Larkin's secretary."

"The Sam Larkin who was your father's political ally? I didn't realize Rebecca was his secretary."

"They called him 'the Kingmaker,' " McConnico said. "You have studied your Arizona history."

"He was a legend."

"And he deserved that label." McConnico said.

The waitress brought the drinks and we both sipped in silence. I was a little surprised that Rebecca had worked for Sam Larkin. I imagined his secretary would have been a severe middle-aged keeper of secrets, and young Rebecca a pretty face in the typing pool. But she was the niece of an important ally. I guess it made some sense.

We talked for maybe an hour, through a so-so meal of "southwestern cuisine." He seemed genuinely curious about how I had put together the threads, missed clues, and hunches involving Rebecca's case. So I gave him the whole drill, from the first trip up to the attic of the old courthouse to my computer work with Lindsey. At the end, his cell phone rang and he had a terse conversation, called for the check, and pulled out his gold card.

"You know, crime is a terrible thing today," McConnico said, setting down his napkin. "What I hear most from my constituents is that they don't feel safe. When we were kids, the only real crime to speak of was the Mafia down in Tucson. Today, we can't keep track of the gangs—Crips, Bloods, that little bastard Bobby Hamid." His voice was suddenly taut with emotion. "When Rebecca was killed, it was a crime that seemed virtually without precedence in Phoenix. Today, it wouldn't even warrant mention on the evening news. Look at how those killings out in the Harquahala Desert seem almost routine now." He shook his head. "My God."

I didn't know if he was trying out a stump speech on me or if he was really speaking from the heart. Considering what had happened to his cousin, I decided to give him the benefit of the doubt.

I got back home just before the long afternoon rush hour started to clot the Valley's streets and freeways. The phone was ringing when I walked in the door; on the other end was a man who said he was Greg Townsend.

Phaedra's lover.

"I, uh, I'm a friend of Phaedra Riding, and I've been trying to find her, and her sister would only tell me that I had to talk to you." He had a well-modulated frat boy's voice.

"When did you last see Phaedra, Mr. Townsend?"

"It would have been in the spring. April, I guess."

"And you haven't seen or spoken to her since then?"

"No," he said. "She needed her space. I wanted to give her that. But we agreed that we'd talk again by the end of June—only she never called."

I tried to decide if I believed him. I told him that a missing person's report had been filed on Phaedra.

"Isn't it unusual for the police to investigate these things unless they suspect foul play?" That struck me as an odd response to being told that his girlfriend had disappeared, but I let it pass.

"Julie and I are old friends. I'm checking into this as a favor to her."

"Well, I hope you'll let me know if I can help in any way," he said. "I'll give you my phone number; it's a Sedona number."

My gut told me I needed to do more to shake something, anything, loose.

"Actually, I'd like to stop by and see you in the next few days, if you can spare a little time?"

"Well," he said. "Is anything wrong? What's going on?"

"I really don't know more than what I've already told you, Mr. Townsend. But if you two were close, you might be able to give me some information that would be helpful. Her family is very concerned."

"Well, sure. Come up tomorrow. Can you be here by nine A.M.?" And then he gave me the address.

Early the next morning, I grabbed a bagel and diet Coke and got on the road to Sedona. I've spent my life in coffee-swilling professions, but I've never caught that addiction. Patty, whose bone-jolting French roast I would brew every morning when we lived together, said I was missing one of life's most sublime pleasures. Maybe it will be like golf: something I'll take up at that ever-receding point in my life called "older." Bagels were something I had discovered, and even if you couldn't find a "real" bagel in Phoenix, I munched contentedly on one as I headed the Blazer north on Black Canyon Freeway, Interstate 17.

Sharon Peralta was on the radio, always "Dr. Sharon" to her listeners (why hadn't I gotten my Ph.D. in psychology?), giving brisk advice to a man who didn't know how to keep his career and meet his obligations to his seven children; a woman who didn't understand why her lovers kept leaving her; and another woman who had seduced her brother-in-law. Dr. Sharon handled every caller deftly. She was funny. She was sexy. She had the answers. She was promoting her newsletter and her new book. Hard to believe it was the mousy Sharon Peralta I first met twenty years ago.

It was a good summer day for a drive, provided you were headed in the right direction. In the southbound lanes, the traffic headed toward downtown was a gridlocked disaster. I drove for miles through the new city sprawl, ever spreading—an acre an hour—out into the desert floor and around stark, barren mountains that once stood in splendid isolation. After passing Carefree Highway, the interstate started to climb. Over the next hundred miles, it would vault nearly six thousand feet into the Arizona high country and Flagstaff. My destination was not quite that far, but no matter how many times I drove this route, I was struck by the dramatic changes in the land.

You can drive all the way from the Mississippi River to Denver without encountering more than the undulating sameness of the plains. In the West, the country changes from pines to deserts and mountains to flatlands with amazing suddenness. So the flat cactus-covered desert gave way to sage- and chaparral-covered slopes, ravines and crevices, all pushing upward toward the high peaks to the north. In a few minutes, the massive blue emptiness of the Bradshaw Mountains appeared off my left. This had been mining country a hundred years before, with lots of abandoned shafts to stick a body in. I felt an involuntary uneasiness and checked the mirrors, checked the .357 in the glove compartment.

In about an hour, I took the highway that splits off north into Oak Creek Canyon and Sedona. Another ten miles and the country changed again from the three-thousand-foot high desert to a landscape from another planet, an idealized Mars of exalted red-stone buttes rising above scrub pines and intricate, blown-apart rock formations, all encased by a gigantic, endless cobalt sky. Here was the next Santa Fe or Taos. Sedona, which had not been much more than an isolated artists' colony when my grandparents would bring me up here as a little boy, had become as rich and exclusive an oasis as you can find in the country. There was now a traffic light below Cathedral Rock and expensive houses sprinkled into the foothills. It all made me vaguely sad.

I stopped at a convenience store where a sign told me Sedona was the home of the annual Jazz on the Rocks Festival, and also that it was at the center of four "vortexes" that provide mysterious, healing energy. I had a vague recollection of a "harmonic convergence" of New Agers here a few years before, when I was still in San Diego and Patty's wicked wit insulated me from inanities. I asked about the address Townsend had given me, and the clerk pointed me down the highway to a turnoff.

The Blazer's odometer turned over 2.4 miles as the asphalt road turned to red gravel and finally to dirt, climbing up into Bear Hollow, a narrow upland canyon overlooking Sedona. Greg Townsend's place was completely concealed in pines and rocks, a modern adobe with the kind of rustic look that can only be had for a lot of money. I parked inside a gate, just behind a silver Porsche 911 turbo. I wondered about strapping on the Python, then decided against it and stepped out onto the pinecones and rocky ground.

"You don't look like a cop," came a disembodied voice from a distance. Then, coming closer, he said, "You look more like a college professor."

Greg Townsend stepped out from behind a boulder and extended his hand. He was tall and lanky, my height, but skinnier, with full a head of graying hair, wire-frame glasses, khaki shorts, and hiking boots. His skin was a golden tan, darker than the color of his shorts. He regarded me with an easy nonchalance in his blue eyes. I pulled out my badge case with my left hand—the nongun hand—and showed it to him.

"I read about you in the *Republic,*" he said. "I'm impressed."

"Nothing to be impressed about," I replied, looking him over and imagining him as Phaedra's lover. I didn't like him.

"I went to Brown, but I never much took to the classroom thing," he said. I didn't respond. "So you're a history professor? I trust you have left behind the prison of linear narrative and the Western conceit that there is such a thing as truth?"

Jesus, I thought, is this how he picked up Phaedra? "I think historical questions have historical answers," I said. "The conceit that everything is relative has led to most of the mass murder of this century."

"Mmm," he said. "How did you ever get tenure?"

He extended his arm and we walked.

"Phaedra loved it up here," he was saying as he led me around the place, from one spectacular view of the canyon below to another. "She was a restless soul. You could see that aura about her. Amazingly creative. Anyway, somehow this place calmed her a bit."

"When was the last time you talked to her, Mr. Townsend?" I asked. We settled onto a large futon in the main room; it faced a wall of glass and another fabulous view. Around us were photos of Townsend climbing, cycling, and skydiving with various young women. I didn't immediately see a photo of Phaedra.

"I told you on the phone, it was April, when she moved out."

"You two had a fight? That was why she moved out?"

His blue eyes flashed for just a moment, and his face became red. "You know," he said, "I didn't want to invite you up here, and now you're asking things that are really not any of your business."

I thought about playing a tough guy, but I just let it sit for a minute. I could hear a siren down in the canyon.

"You didn't know Phaedra," Townsend said. "The negativity just grew in her. She was very difficult, very tumultuous. Of course, she was very bright and talented. They all go together. Such a tortured soul.

"Yes, we fought before she left. But that didn't seem unusual, because we fought a lot. That was just Phaedra. But the next morning, she was just gone. She never gave me an explanation."

"Why do you think she left?"

He shrugged. "Maybe she was ready for a change. She lived a very episodic life, Deputy Mapstone. She would go through phases in her clothes: hats and loose skirts one month, tight Armani cocktail dresses the next. People came and went, too, men especially. She never had trouble turning the page."

"What did her state of mind seem to be?"

"Moody. Sometimes she seemed happy, but lonely, too."

"And other times?"

"She never reached a oneness with herself. That wonderful state of being I tried to teach her. Why should I know why?" He sounded whiny, like he must have sounded in fifth grade.

"Oh, just because you lived with her," I said dryly.

"Yeah," he said, staring past me out the window. "There were times she sounded really down. She could have the blackest moods. And that sister . . ."

"Julie."

He looked at me strangely and said, "Very bad news."

"Did you ever have any sense she might be in trouble?"

He shook his head. We watched as a hawk hunted in a lonely arc down the canyon.

I asked him about how he'd met Phaedra.

"The personals, Deputy Mapstone. Or is it Dr. Mapstone? Professor? Haven't you tried the nineties way of meeting people?"

"I answered a couple of ads in San Diego a few years ago. I can't say I met anybody like Phaedra, at least if her photos don't lie."

"Oh my God, she looked much better in person," Townsend said. "She was the kind of woman who, when you saw her walk past or in an elevator, could make your whole day if she gave you a smile.

"I've known a woman or two like that," I said.

"I've never seen anyone who was vibrating as high as Phaedra. She was channeling unbelievable things . . ." He stopped and looked at me. "But I guess you don't believe in such things, do you, Professor Mapstone?"

" 'There are more things in heaven and earth, Horatio, than are dreamt of in your philosophy,' " I said.

"The Bible," he said, and smiled.

I thought, Shakespeare, you dolt. I said, "But I guess I don't channel."

"You should. You have quite an aura about you. It would allow you to break free of all the repressiveness of Western civilization and Christianity, which, thank God, nobody believes in anymore."

"Yeah. The Sedona vortex is certainly more plausible than the Trinity." He didn't smile. "Phaedra," I coaxed.

"She didn't like to climb. Heights scared her. She read books. Lots of history. You might have liked her."

He was needling me, but I let him. There was something wrong with Greg Townsend, but I couldn't tell if it was that vague misfit neurosis that seems to migrate west or if it was something more, something to do with Phaedra.

"I had a place down in the Valley," he said. "So we started dating down there. It got serious, and we moved in together. Then we moved up here full-time."

"What do you do for a living, Mr. Townsend?"

"I'm a trust baby, Deputy."

"Must be nice."

"Yes, it allows me to do the things I love. I climb at least a dozen fourteeners every year; I fly my own plane; I travel. And I can attract women like Phaedra Riding, to put a fine point on it."

He smiled a smile of perfect white teeth.

"Did you care about her?"

"Sure," he said. "We had a lot of fun."

"I can see you're broken up with worry about her disappearing," I said.

He looked hard at me for a long moment. The veins and tendons in his fine neck rippled minutely. "You don't know anything about me."

"I know you don't seem too concerned."

He just stared and gave a little sigh. "I don't have to justify myself to you," he said. "She's an adult, and one with her own mind, let me assure you. She liked being on her own. I have no reason to believe she won't turn up."

"Did Phaedra have a drug problem?"

"Fuck you!" he said, rising and stalking to the end of the room. He walked over to a bar set into the wall and clinked some ice into a glass. It seemed out of character; I expected him to be swilling Evian. "I really didn't have to let you in here, and I don't have to let you pry into my life."

I stayed seated. "Well, that's true, sir," I said. "So I can call the Sedona sheriff's substation and get a search warrant and really fuck up your afternoon. To put a fine point on it."

He downed his drink. I said, "Or we can keep having a friendly conversation."

"She hated drugs," he said quietly, staring out the window again.

I drove back to Phoenix in the full heat of the day, the sun burning into the Blazer despite the air-conditioning being on high. My sunglasses were pressed tightly against my face. I missed San

Diego. I missed the Spanish stucco house a block from the Pacific in Ocean Beach. I missed the familiarity of lecture classes Mondays, Wednesdays, and Fridays, and office hours Wednesday afternoons, and lunch with Patty in Mission Valley, where the air was cool and salty-smelling.

Here, I had a missing woman who had a taste for rich men, couldn't keep a job, and played the personal ads. She had red hair and a blue Nissan Sentra, and I didn't have a clue where to find her. Who would have thought it would be easier to solve a four-decades-old murder case than to find my old girlfriend's missing sister?

I didn't know what to think about Greg Townsend, aside from my visceral dislike of him. He was like so many middle-aged men you meet in the West, grown-up boys who have left behind the privileged Ivy League backgrounds, but not the perks. Men who try to fill up what is missing inside them with mountain biking, rock climbing, and New Age philosophy. They populated the resorts and the tennis ranches, looking like they've stepped out of a Tommy Hilfiger ad in *Esquire* magazine. They have a finely tuned sense of ironic scorn, but it's impossible to say if they ever feel anything real. And what Townsend felt about Phaedra, I couldn't say.

There was a screeching in the console, and I remembered the cellular phone Peralta had given me last week. I pulled it out and activated it.

"Mapstone." It was Peralta. "Where the hell have you been? What's your ten-twenty?"

Nobody had spoken radio code to me for fifteen years. "I'm just south of Black Canyon City on I-Seventeen."

"Get on I-Ten," he commanded. "Head out past the White Tanks to Tonopah, then follow the dirt road three miles." I told him to slow down, then grabbed a pad and wrote it down.

"What's up?" I asked. But somehow I already knew.

"We found your girl," Peralta said, his voice cutting in and out. "Phaedra, like Phoenix."

I knew what he meant. But he said it anyway.

"Body dump."

It is more than a hundred miles from the edge of the Valley's civilizing sprawl to the Colorado River and the border of California. Today, Interstate 10 runs through it like a straightedge, connecting Los Angeles with its ambitious New West offspring, Phoenix. But on both sides of the freeway is some of the most desolate territory on the planet. The La Posa Plain, the Ranegras Plain, the Kofa Wilderness. The abandoned bed of a long-lost inland sea. Bounded on both sides by bare, ragged mountains with names like Eagletail Peak, Signal Mountain, and Fourth of July Butte. Until the mid-1970s, even travelers between Phoenix and L.A. avoided these badlands. The railroad ran south and west, through Yuma, or north and west through Wickenburg. The old highway took an out-of-the-way route north, for otherwise there would have been no towns and no water for travelers. And even now, with all our mastery of nature, with all of Phoenix's seemingly invincible growth, the Harquahala Desert is a forbidding place.

I drove for an hour on freeways, first south into the city and then west into the sun. I slowed down to let a dust devil twist across the interstate, knowing these whirlwinds were capable of overturning tractor-trailer rigs. At the little hamlet of Tonopah, I got onto surface streets and then dirt roads as the last subdivisions gave way to scattered ranch houses and then trailers and finally nothing but chaparral and cactus amid the endless cracked blond dirt of the desert. I played the CD Lindsey had given me and then I sat in silence. A sheet of sweat would not evaporate from my skin.

I tried not to think, but of course I did. By the time I'd left the Sheriff's Office years ago, I had built the necessary nonchalance about finding dead bodies. But it hadn't always been that way. There was the night I was a twenty-year-old rookie serving a warrant with Peralta to an old hotel in the Deuce and finding a forgotten dead man instead. Peralta called it "a stinker." I stumbled back down the stairs and onto the street, vomiting my dinner onto the hot sidewalk. For years, I had been ashamed of that, but at least it was human.

There were dusty sheriff's cruisers on both sides of the trail. I parked behind the last one, adjusted my sunglasses, and stepped out into the heat. It was like walking into an oven set on high, under a brilliant blue sky, with a cactus wren cooing off in the distance.

"You Mapstone?" a young deputy asked. I said I was and showed my ID. She nodded and led me off into the desert. We walked maybe a quarter of a mile, over soil hard and ancient, down a wash and back up into a thicket of mesquite and cholla, which was now roped off with crime-scene tape that looked weirdly out of place here. Tall uniformed men in sunglasses milled around. I pulled out my badge and hung it on my belt, feeling strangely at home.

"She hasn't been here long," Peralta said. He was wearing jeans and a T-shirt with the logo MCSO CHAIN GANG—one of the sheriff's marketing coups—his Glock 9-mm pistol restraining his belly. He led me under the tape. We were careful to walk single file in case other footprints might be found around the scene.

"What do you mean?" I said. "She disappeared a month ago."

"Look," he said. Suddenly, we were there, beside a small bluff, under a creosote bush, pulling back a plastic blanket, looking at a pale, red-haired young woman.

Peralta read my mind. "Nobody looks that good if they've been in the desert six days, much less six weeks. I think she was dumped in the last few hours."

I asked, "Who found her?" but I was hardly listening when Peralta said, “Anonymous call to the nine one one operator.” I was looking at Phaedra. Her eyes were still staring, dead now, at whoever had killed her and brought her here. I did not know her. And yet I did.

“David.” Peralta was next to me. “You okay?”

I nodded.

He pulled down the plastic sheet. “Looks like strangulation of some kind. Note the marks on the neck—may be consistent with a utility cord or some kind of climbing rope. Only wearing a bra when she was found. Her purse had ID and fifty dollars inside. Sexual abuse not determined. Crime lab is on the way from Phoenix.”

“What about her hands?” I said. “Check under her nails.”

“Thank you, professor,” Peralta said, annoyed.

I stood a bit uncertainly and stared off at a mountain in the distance, a redoubt for the apocalypse if you could only get water to it. “It's like Stokes,” I said.

“Huh?” Peralta said.

“The bra. Only wearing a bra. Strangled. They'll find she was raped, too. Like Rebecca Stokes and Leslie Reeves and Ginger Brocato and Betty Moran and Gloria Johnson. It's the same way those homicides were done.”

Peralta pulled me aside, pulled off his sunglasses. His brown eyes were rimmed with red cracks. “This is now and this is another Harquahala murder,” he said.

I felt like he'd kicked me in the stomach.

“What are you saying?” I said. “The Harquahala murders have been prostitutes, dumped in the desert. This isn't that.”

He only looked at me. I grabbed his shoulder.

“This isn't that, Mike. This is Phaedra Riding.”

“You don't know who Phaedra was,” Peralta said. “You didn't know her secrets. From what you told me, she sounded like a flake.” It was too hot for long sentences.

“She wasn't turning tricks.”

“You don't know. You're too close to this.”

“I know that much.”

“You need to let the homicide guys handle this now.”

“I was the only one who cared about this case until today.”

He looked down at my hand on his collarbone. I didn't even realize it was there. I let it fall.

"You are not on the case," he said. "This is now going to the Harquahala task force." He pointed to some men in white polo shirts and tan chinos walking the perimeter and looking at me with some hostility. "You stick to the historic cases, partner."

I walked away from him and knelt down by Phaedra, a rag doll on the dry ground. I tried to make myself look at her as an investigator. I covered her up too gently. Peralta's hand was on my shoulder.

"If you want to help, you can tell her sister and then drive her downtown to make a statement," he said. "And I want a report from you on what you know about her." I stood.

"But that's it. Otherwise, I want you to stay away from this."

I appeared in the posh marketing office of the Phoenician covered with sweat, my badge still hanging from my belt. I was wearing the kind of grim expression that caused a graduate assistant a few years ago to call to me "ponderous." Julie came out to meet me, and I'm sure she knew immediately. But I silently led her out to the opulent lobby.

"You know, Charlie Keating built this place," she said, talking a little too fast. "That was all while you were away. Then the feds took it over in the S and L crash. Then they sold it to a Saudi sheik." She waved her arm vaguely. "It's like a palace. First-class all the way. The finest hotel in Phoenix. Even better than the Biltmore, I think."

The room felt very large around me. I said, "I have bad news."

"We've won five stars from the *Mobil Guide* every year, you know," she went on, smiling. "That's very hard to do. God, when it comes time every year to announce the rankings, I get so nervous."

"It's Phaedra."

She stopped talking and stared into her lap. She did a double take and her eyes filled with tears, which she anxiously rubbed away. Then she just seemed to collapse in a heap of choked sobs and melting mascara.

"I'm sorry, Julie. We found her body. I am so sorry."

She was silent, rigid, and she stayed in my arms until my back began to ache from being turned the wrong way, but I didn't move. Then I drove her downtown in a silence broken only by the strained noise of the Blazer's air-conditioning on high. First to the morgue, then to the station. While she met with the detectives, I wandered around the building. It was after 5:00 P.M. now, and the place had that feel of weekend institutional abandonment that I remembered from universities. Closed, dark offices. Peralta's door was closed and locked. Lindsey wasn't in Records. I left her a note saying hi; I don't know why. I bought a diet Coke and went back to CID to cool my heels.

How do we arrive at life, real life? Would Dr. Sharon have the answer? For years, I imagined Julie had found a neurosurgeon and was making perfect babies in a house overlooking the Bay in San Francisco, working on her tennis swing and managing the family portfolio. But that didn't take into account life's misfires, did it? Like how I was going to be the great writer of popular history, the next Simon Schama or Paul Johnson. Inspire people. Make money, too. Live on a hillside in La Jolla with my beautiful, witty wife and my books and my big thoughts. Live as far away from crime-scene tape and body bags and next-of-kin notification that I could ever get. Like how Phaedra Riding came home to Phoenix to start her whole life over and ended up dead instead. This was real life, straight up.

After about an hour, Julie came out grim-faced and red-eyed. One of the detectives, a guy named Grady, I think, told me they were done with her, and then he closed the door in my face when I started to follow him back inside. It could have pissed me off, but I was concerned about Julie. We walked out in silence. When the elevator reached the first floor, she said, "Please buy me a drink." I needed one, too.

"That detective kept asking me whether Phaedra had ever been involved in prostitution," Julie was saying. "He wouldn't tell me why; he just kept coming back to that. What's going on, David?" She was more angry than hurt, nervously swirling the ice around in her scotch.

"And Peralta wonders why I don't want to be a cop again," I said half to myself. "Phaedra was found in the desert west of the city, where they have found the bodies of several murdered prostitutes over the past eighteen months. Those detectives are part of a task force working on the Harquahala murders."

"Wait a minute!" Julie nearly shrieked, causing some people at nearby tables to look up. We were at a restaurant in the Arizona Center, a tony commercial office development a few blocks away from the Sheriff's Administration Building office. Then, in a lower voice, she said, "What are you talking about? Phaedra was not a prostitute!"

"I know that."

"Then why are you letting them do that?"

"Well, they're not exactly clamoring for my input, Julie," I said, nursing a martini. "They have to assume the worst because of where the body was found."

It was as if I had physically struck her; she recoiled.

" 'The body.' That's my sister."

"I'm sorry. It's an old habit. A bad one."

Julie excused herself for a long trip to the rest room. I sipped the martini and looked out at the palm trees swaying. A storm was coming into town. Maybe we would get an hour's break from the monotonous heat.

When she returned, I asked, "Julie, I need to know if there's more to this than you've told me."

"What do you mean?"

"I mean, have you told me everything?" Like when you slept with Jim Ellis after that party when we were juniors but never told me. "We don't know yet for sure, but it seems obvious that Phaedra was alive until very recently. So where was she? Had she been in danger all this time? Had she disappeared voluntarily, or was she kidnapped? What about those men who were watching you? Is there anything you haven't told me?"

She shook her head, then said, "Sometimes Phaedra would just go away for a while, but never like this. It was her way of just shutting down when relationships or whatever got too intense. She might not let Mom and Dad know, but she'd always let me know."

"Should you notify your mom?"

Julie's eyes darkened and she shook her head vehemently. "You know, in a weird way, you're lucky you never knew your parents, David. And I know how alone you must feel now that your grandparents are gone. But they did love you. I can't say my folks ever loved any of us."

She swirled the golden liquid in her glass. "We were the perfect family." She laughed unhappily. "Once, when I was about fifteen, I was out with some friends and we ran into Dad with his girlfriend. He'd screwed around for years, I guess. But that's kind of hard to handle when you're fifteen. Finally, he just left and never came back. Moved to Florida. Married a bimbo. Not that it really mattered, because when I was growing up, he never had anything to offer but slaps and criticism. Nothing I ever did was enough to earn his love."

I let the waitress refill our glasses. It had been years since I'd heard Julie talk about her father, but the bitterness was undimmed. Hers was a ghost-ridden family drowning in what Sharon Peralta would call "unresolved sorrows." A brother killed himself when he was seventeen.

"Mom was useless," Julie said. "Pills and booze. She was worse after the divorce. And "—she choked a bit—" Phaedra got the worst of it. Phaedra always felt that abandonment, so she was determined never to trust, always to be the first to leave."

Outside, a sparse rain was starting to fall, hitting the palm trees with big dusty drops. It made me feel a little better. Even a little change from the constant oppression of the heat was welcome.

"I'm so tired, David," she said, and she looked it. "I don't know what else to tell you right now."

We drank in silence. Then we walked through the dust and lightning back to the Blazer and I started to drive her to her car. Instead, we ended up at my place, where we drank too much. She cried a long time, then finally came to my bed, where we made love with the peculiar frenzy of the lost and the grief-stricken.

I am running through *my neighborhood in the eternal twilight of dreams. All the houses are familiar but darkened, and I can't run fast enough to catch up with Phaedra. She has always just been there before I arrive. And she is in danger. I know this. And I run into my house, thinking I will find Mother and Dad and Grandma and Grandfather, and there is so much I need to tell them now, now that I'm a forty-year-old man.*

But the house is empty except for the twilight, the loneliest part of the day, the lonely Sunday night of the clock. But then I know I'm not alone, and I see someone, and I know we are in danger. And I fire the Python and watch as the bullet moves too slowly, too slowly, and falls to the floor.

And then I am in bed, my legs entangled in Phaedra's legs, exhausted from lovemaking. She laughs when she makes love. She runs that red hair across my chest. The neighbors keep pounding, pounding on the wall, but we laugh and don't care.

The door. I sat up and pulled away from Julie, who was still out. I looked back again. Julie Riding in my bed. Last night had really happened. I pulled on a robe and walked to the front of the house. Peralta was at the door. The clock on the wall said 2:15—in the afternoon.

"Goddamn it, I've been banging on the door for fifteen minutes," Peralta said, walking past me. "You never used to be a heavy sleeper."

"Good morning to you, too." God, my head hurt.

"It was a shitty morning, and now it's a shitty afternoon. You have any coffee? Oh, shit, do you still not drink coffee?"

He was wearing a dark blue suit and a crisp white shirt, a grim expression on his face. I offered to make some coffee.

"I will." It was Julie. She appeared in the hallway, wearing my ASU T-shirt.

"Julie." Peralta waved a little wave. He seemed uncharacteristically awkward.

"Hello, Mike. Just like old times, isn't it?" She ran a hand through her tangled brown-blond hair and padded into the kitchen. Peralta arched an eyebrow at me and nodded toward the living room.

"Where were you yesterday morning when I called you on the cell phone?" Peralta sat heavily into the sofa.

"I went up to Sedona to see Phaedra's old boyfriend. I thought he might have a clue as to where she was."

"And what made you do that?"

"What's going on, Mike?" I began, but his look caught me short. "He called me the night before."

Peralta sighed heavily. "Greg Townsend was found dead this morning."

"What?"

"You heard me, David. Murdered. His cleaning lady found him this morning in the bedroom at his place in Sedona. He'd apparently been tortured with a raw electrical chord before he was given the business end of a twelve gauge. The Coconino County deputies found your name and phone number written on a pad on his desk. And naturally, they wanted to know what a Maricopa County deputy had been doing on their turf."

I sat carefully in the leather easy chair. I told Peralta what Townsend had told me.

"Goddamn it, David, I told you to stay out of this case!" He was headed to the blowup point, which I didn't want to see.

"It wasn't anything but a missing persons case when I talked to Townsend, and you gave me permission to look into that. Remember?"

Julie walked in with coffee for Peralta and herself and a diet Coke for me. I patted her hand.

"Julie, sit." It was Peralta. "I'm really sorry about your sister. But I have to ask you this. Where were you yesterday before David brought you downtown?"

"Is this an interrogation, Mike?" She tossed her hair a bit and sat opposite me. Her eyes were red and puffy.

Peralta sipped the coffee. "Good coffee," he said, then: "It can be if you want. Should I read you your rights?"

"Wait a minute, Mike," I said. "I picked her up at the Phoenician, where she works."

I turned to Julie and said, "Greg Townsend was found murdered." Peralta shot me a dirty look.

"I didn't kill him, Mike, if that's what you're asking," Julie said. "Not that I hadn't thought about it, the way he treated Phaedra."

"Julie! Jesus."

Peralta said, "I think you should come downtown with me and talk to us about this."

"Are you arresting me, Mike? Is that easier than looking for the son of a bitch who murdered my sister?"

He finished the coffee and stood. "David will be happy to drive you down when you two, uh, finish here."

I was supposed to lecture at Phoenix College that afternoon. Instead, I canceled class to take Julie back to Madison Street. Not that I had taken any time to prepare the lecture. Not that I had made much progress on anything. I was no closer to selling the house than I had been two months ago. I was no closer to getting a new job. What I had accomplished was to land in this strange little drama with characters out of my past—my old partner, my old girlfriend. And the drama had a body count that was rising.

I spent a frustrating hour being interrogated by two young detectives from the Harquahala task force, who wanted to argue over every sentence in my report on Phaedra. One kept reminding me that he had a master's degree.

They went away, and I logged into the sheriff's computer and read a fragmentary report from the Coconino County deputies on Greg Townsend, who was now neither vibrating nor channeling. It sounded very ugly. Blood on the walls, literally. And the place was just isolated enough that nobody was likely to have heard a thing. Suspect number one in Phaedra's murder was dead himself, leaving nothing. Maybe the Harquahala task force would make sense of it. Maybe I could let it all go. Let Julie make another statement, straighten out her whereabouts yesterday. And I could get back to my life.

"Hello, History Shamus." It was Lindsey. Her black miniskirt was even shorter than usual. She looked me over. "You look like you were out all night. I hope sex was involved."

I could feel the blood rushing to my face. She gave a me conspiratorial smile. "Way to go, Dave." I showed her the report from Sedona.

"Shit," she whispered. "He pissed somebody off. Execution city. Are you involved in this?"

"It's a long story," I said. "He's some guy who dated the little sister of an old friend of mine. The little sister turned up dead yesterday."

"Phaedra," Lindsey said. I nodded.

"I saw the report come through. Neat name. The daughter of Minos."

I smiled at her. "Lindsey, you are always full of surprises."

"I've read Racine," she said with an endearing smugness. "This Phaedra found a world of trouble, too. It's been assigned to the Harquahala task force."

I nodded.

"Was she turning tricks?"

"No," I said. "I don't think it's one of the Harquahala killings."

Lindsey looked at me quizzically.

"I know this sounds nuts, Lindsey. But something about this isn't right. Peralta called me out to the scene yesterday to identify Phaedra's body. And it was like she had just been murdered."

"One would think that would be enough," Lindsey said.

"Her body, the crime scene, they had been"—I searched for the right word—" 'arranged.' Like serial-killer performance art. It was the same way the bodies were found back in the late 1950s."

"You're getting weird on me, Dave."

"You read the reports. You'll see it."

There was a detective standing in the doorway. "Mapstone." He cocked his head toward the hall. "Chief Peralta wants you." He turned and walked away.

Lindsey pulled me close to whisper, "I'm glad you're not one of those knuckle-draggers." Her dark shoulder-length hair was very soft.

Peralta hunched down in his big chair, head propped on his hands, staring at a can of caffeine-free diet Coke, gnawing his cuticle. He didn't look at me when I came in.

Then, in a little high-pitched sneer, he said, " 'Oh, gee, Sharon, Julie and I are just friends now.' "

"We are," I said. "Sometimes things happen between friends, especially during times of stress." My head was throbbing. I sat down. "Not that it's any of your business."

"It is my business, since you are a Maricopa County deputy," Peralta said. "And you've really stepped in some shit here. Two bodies in two days. Julie can't account for her whereabouts when Townsend was killed. And when I come by to ask you about it, she's climbing out of your goddamned bed. I thought I'd been sent back twenty years in time."

"It was a case you didn't give a shit about, Mike. While we're digging up unfortunate quotes of the past month, I recall a certain chief deputy saying something like 'Phaedra's just shacking up with some guy and she'll turn up.' Now you're acting like I somehow created this situation."

His eyes darkened visibly and I knew I was in for it. But he just sighed and leaned back in his chair. Up came his legs, and his fine lizard-skin boots claimed the desktop.

"I suppose you have a hypothesis?" he asked.

"I thought this belonged to the task force." I didn't have a clue.

"It does, for now. But Townsend complicates things. If he was Phaedra's lover, it's hard to believe it was just a coincidence. There were thousands of dollars' worth of art and electronics in his house up there, and it was all left. This was no robbery gone wrong. Maybe big sister decided to give paybacks to little sister's nasty-boy lover."

"Wait a minute." My head was spinning. I vowed never to take another drink as long as I lived. "When was Townsend murdered?"

"Best guess until the lab work comes back is yesterday afternoon. Probably not long after you left."

"So you're saying Julie already knew Phaedra was dead, drove at ninety miles an hour to Sedona to ice this guy, turned around and drove at ninety miles an hour to get back to the hotel so she could be there when I told her about finding her sister's body?"

Peralta's face tightened. "I don't know what I think," he said. "Something's not right about this, David."

"Have you gotten lab work back on Phaedra?"

Peralta shook his head. "The medical examiner takes his time because he knows this thing is going to be seen by everybody, including the feds. Hell, it only happened half a mile from the La Paz County line, so I've got this little-town Buford Pusser busting my chops. And it's only a matter of time before the *Republic* starts doing more on this serial killer than the isolated stories about the body of a suspected prostitute turning up in the desert."

My stomach did a little free fall. "What did the evidence technicians find?"

Peralta looked disgusted. "They didn't find dick."

"The car? Blue Nissan Sentra?"

He shook his head. "Nothing."

I walked over to his little refrigerator and got a diet Coke. I sipped it cautiously. "Mike, answer me this: How many times before did your Harquahala killer call the Communications Center to say where a body could be found?"

"None."

"Have the others been this close to La Paz County?"

"No, no, goddamn it. But what does that prove? Green River crossed county lines. Ramirez did Orange County and L.A. County—hell, even San Francisco. None of these guys can read a map 'cause they're too busy talking to Satan or their neighbor's terrier."

"And did the MO of the body dump jibe?"

Peralta sighed again.

"It didn't, did it?"

"We can't be sure," Peralta said. "He changes his routine every time. He's not as ritualistic as some I've seen. Look, David, even if she wasn't turning tricks, we don't know what we're dealing with yet. By your own report, Phaedra answered personal ads, had lots of men in her life. Who knows who she met out there."

"Come on, Mike! Most people who answer personal ads don't end up dead. You know this isn't related. You're just letting this thing run on bureaucratic momentum. If I didn't know better, I'd think you were trying to group some homicides so when you get your Harquahala killer, you'll have a higher clearance rate."

"Okay, hotshot. What's your theory?"

I sat back down and sipped the cold drink. "I don't have one yet. But I have a strange feeling about it."

Peralta looked at me.

"She was meant to be found. Most body dumps, the killer hopes the victim won't be found. This guy calls nine one one and gives directions. And she was meant to be found in a certain way, just like those women forty years ago."

Peralta threw up his hands. "This shit again."

"Hear me out," I said. "So he's a media junkie. He read about Stokes, saw you and me on TV. Wanted to make a point."

"What point?" Peralta fairly shouted. "Why would he even know you knew Phaedra from Adam? And how do we know he didn't grab her weeks before the story broke about the Stokes case?"

"I don't know," I said. "I don't know yet."

* * *

Two days passed. Julie and I holed up at my house like two hermits in winter. Only we were hiding from the sun and the heat and our own heartbreaks. We made love and held each other. It was both familiar and strange, as if we had always been together and yet we were only touching copies of our sensual selves from long ago. The oleanders and citrus trees protected us from the world for a while.

We talked more. Julie slowly filled in some of the blanks of her life: She married a lawyer named Royce. He beat her up at least once a month. They went to a lot of parties and did a lot of cocaine. They had a daughter. When Julie finally grew sick of the beatings and the husband's affairs, she sued him for divorce. Royce got custody of the daughter, Mindy, after a protracted fight. "He went to law school with the judge, for God's sake," she said. Then a couple of aimless years—"I went kind of crazy when I lost Mindy"—spent with a succession of bad-news lovers. Then some therapy. Now, she was trying to get her life back together, maybe get the court to modify the custody award. And was dealing with the death of her younger sister. There was nothing for me to do but listen.

At night, I slept fitfully, the .357 just under the bed, the outside noises casting sinister echoes. Julie burrowed deep against me, pulling my arm across her body, nesting her feet against my legs. Sometimes I would wake up and hear her sobbing softly, and I would hold her closer.

In the daytime, we wandered off separately for our lonely rituals. I tried to read some, write some, keep my mind distracted. Books had never been a comfort to Julie, so she watched daytime TV and drank alone, until she couldn't stand it any longer. Then she came and wrapped me up in her arms, trembling and sobbing.

On Saturday, I woke up from a five-fathom-deep sleep and the other side of the bed was empty. The phone was ringing and the clock said five minutes ahead of noon. When I picked it up, the line was silent. And then a deep voice said, "Mapstone. This is Harrison Wolfe. Detective Harrison Wolfe, Phoenix PD, retired. I think we need to have a talk."

Palm Lane took me east through monotonous, declining neighborhoods of cinder-block ranch houses and lawns of dying grass. Not a dog, cat, or human ventured into the midsummer heat. Forty years ago, when Phoenix became a city of several hundred thousand nearly overnight, these homes symbolized the American dream. The vets came west to live in endless sunshine and work at places like Motorola and Sperry Rand. Builders like Del Webb and John F. Long would put them in a house for twelve thousand dollars on a VA loan.

Block after block, mile after mile, the subdivisions took over the lettuce fields and citrus groves. Now the speed, volume, and thrift with which the houses had been thrown up was only too apparent. The old owners had long ago moved to newer neighborhoods, leaving thousands of seedy rentals, the homely ghosts of 1950s dreams. Gang graffiti sat everywhere, defiant and ugly. Cars leaked oil into yards once lovingly tended. A Sun Belt slum, crumbling and rusting and dying under the relentless sun. It salted my black mood, made me hate Phoenix all over again and vow to get out as soon as I could.

At Twenty-fourth Street, I turned south and found the little taqueria where Harrison Wolfe had said he would meet me. It sat in an old Circle K building, another soulless cinder-block relic from "old" Phoenix. I parked the Blazer next to half a dozen low-riders.

Inside, I was the only Anglo in the place. I ordered a Negra Modelo in Spanish and sat in a corner booth, feeling everyone's eyes on me.

When the old Anglo walked in, I knew it had to be Wolfe. The machismo in the young Mexican-American men milling around the jukebox just seemed to die, and they sullenly shrank away from him. He was tall, slender, and ramrod-straight, and he was wearing a crisp white shirt, jeans, and cowboy boots. As he looked at me, I took in his craggy, sunburned face, his shock of white hair. He must have been a handsome man once, but he had cop's eyes, narrow and searching. And although he walked stiffly, his movements held the confidence of potential violence. He sat carefully across from me, did not extend his hand or greet me in any way. When he had settled, he fixed blue eyes on me.

"So you're the great history professor who's been investigating the Rebecca Stokes case."

"So you're the little lady who started the great war," I could hear Lincoln say as he greeted Harriet Beecher Stowe. I met Wolfe's eyes, knowing that to have done so years ago would have meant a sudden visit from the sap or the club. Cold blue eyes in a face ruined by age and the sun.

"Yes, I found some new information," I said.

A slender girl with black hair down to her waist brought him two shots of tequila and a plate of enchiladas. He downed both shots, one after another, and started eating. I drank the Negra Modelo, feeling a sour knot growing in my stomach.

"Nobody in the department even knows you're still alive," I ventured. He had to be at least eighty.

He looked at me sourly and mopped up salsa with a large tortilla.

"I don't want the bastards to know where I am." He signaled for more tequila. "I would have been happy never to see another cop in my life. Just another old man tossing bread to the pigeons at Encanto Lagoon, which is all Mexicans now anyway."

I started to talk, but he cut me off with a look.

"I was the first full-time homicide investigator in the Phoenix Police Department," he said. "It's hard to believe, but nobody now can appreciate how small the town was just a few years ago. I got my start in L.A., then came over here as a sergeant in 1950. I was a personal friend of Chief Parker. I could have done anything. But my wife had tuberculosis. The dry air was better for her. Hell, there was no smog then."

The young men had left, and we were alone with the smell of grease and tortillas and the soft clink of dishes in the kitchen.

"When those girls turned up dead, we'd never had anything like that here. The patrol officers, the brass, they didn't know what to do. Hell, we didn't even know what we were dealing with at first. The only thing that had happened in Phoenix up to that point was Winnie Ruth Judd back in the thirties, and that was just a love triangle. When Ginger Brocato turned up in the desert, we went looking for an old boyfriend, somebody who knew her. We looked for the obvious. It only dawned on us slowly that we were dealing with a psycho who killed randomly."

I put the beer bottle down and studied his face. It revealed nothing.

He went on, counting on arthritic fingers. "Ginger, Leslie Reeves, and Gloria Johnson were the work of Eddie Evans. Very good."

And that was more Lindsey's work than anything, I thought.

"Betty Moran was Evans and a partner, a little two-bit burglar named Felix Hernandez, who tagged along with Eddie one night and got in over his head."

"If you knew this, why didn't you arrest him?"

"Look, Ivory Tower, I didn't know. Nobody knew until Felix Hernandez got scared and came to us. I knew it was the work of one man. But he was smart, careful. No fingerprints. Not even a partial. He didn't seem to have any patterns, except for choosing young women with fair hair who were alone. And he didn't make any of the mistakes that solve most cases, like getting his car ticketed sitting outside the murder scene. No, we didn't have squat until Felix started singing."

"But Evans never went to jail."

"Let me tell you something. We went to his place, a little apartment off Seventh Street and Garfield. Nobody home. We stake it out. And over the radio, we hear a call about a knife fight down in the Deuce. Then they broadcast the victim's name: Eddie Evans."

He ate a forkful of enchilada. "I guess I could have figured it was a kind of rough justice, like the God of the Old Testament reaching out to get this bastard. But I didn't. I wanted him so bad. I wanted to know. Know why he did it. How he got away from us all those years. It was the worst night of my life."

"Was any of this ever put in a report?"

He shook his head. "I wrote it all down and the county attorney took the reports. I never saw them again. Other cases came along. Life goes on."

"And Stokes?"

"Not connected."

My day was getting a lot worse. "How can you be so sure?"

"I know. It sure as hell wasn't Eddie Evans, because I had him on ice the week she disappeared."

"That wasn't in his file."

" 'His file,' " Harrison Wolfe spat out. " 'The report.' That's why I left the cops. We were turned into bureaucrats and pencil pushers. Where some teacher"—he looked at me hard—"can walk in and claim to clear old cases, working for the sheriff no less. Let me ask you something, bookworm. Do you trust Napoléon's *Correspondence* if you're a historian?"

"No," I stuttered, surprised. "He was writing from Saint Helena with his reputation in mind."

"Well, there you go. And that's what most cops are doing: covering ass. I never wrote an arrest report on the little creep because I couldn't charge him. Today, he'd have a lawyer and the ACLU down our throats. Back then, we had some discretion. Some latitude."

"But Stokes had the same MO as the other girls."

Wolfe shook his head. "The Stokes girl was raped and strangled and dumped in the desert. But not the way Eddie would do it." He held up a hand. "Don't go asking for the report. Nobody ever wrote down the way Eddie mutilated and tortured those girls before he killed them. He was a monster."

"So Eddie wasn't the Creeper? Or the Creeper didn't kill Stokes, either?"

"Eddie may have been the Creeper," Wolfe said. "I think he was. But neither one killed Rebecca.

"You see"—he polished off the food and wiped his face roughly with a napkin—"the worst thing an investigator can do is confuse his instincts with his prejudices. You work a hundred murder cases and they're all the same. So you're tempted to think murder one hundred and one is the same, too. That's where you screw up. Because there're a million reasons why people end up dead. A million secrets behind those dead eyes. And nothing keeps secrets better than the desert.

"No." He shook his head. "Rebecca Stokes was killed by somebody she knew."

I drove with no destination, just to be moving. Out to the Squaw Peak Parkway and north toward the mountains in the clot of rush-hour traffic. I called Peralta on the cellular phone, but his secretary said he had gone to a Mounted Posse awards dinner. I tried Julie at my house and at her home, but there was no answer. Lindsey's voice answered her phone, but it was only her answering machine. I didn't leave a message.

Harry Truman said the only thing new in the world is the history you don't know. Harrison Wolfe had lived some of that history. And I was drowning in what I didn't know. I didn't know who had killed Rebecca Stokes. I didn't know who had killed Phaedra Riding or where she had been for the month since she disappeared. I didn't know why Phaedra's killer would want to copy what he thought was the MO of the Stokes case. I didn't know why Greg Townsend was dead or how that was related to Phaedra. And I didn't know the secrets that the desert was hiding from me.

The phone rang at 1:45 the next morning. It was Julie.

"David," she said. "Do you know I really love you? I've always loved you."

"I—"

"You are so kind, David. You turned into such a fine man. I never doubted it. I just haven't had much experience with men like you in my life." She laughed unhappily.

"Where are you, Julie?"

"I have to go away, my love. Please don't ask questions. I think we're in great danger. I have to do this, David."

There was something in her voice—a peculiar trill.

"Do what, Julie?"

"David, please don't ask right now. We're in danger."

I asked her why we were in danger.

"Phaedra's dead." Her voice went up a notch. "Greg is dead. I can't talk now."

"Julie, Peralta is not going to like this. You could be a material witness in a capital murder case."

"Fuck him." She laughed. "I'll be in touch."

The line went dead.

I replaced the receiver as if it were a live bomb. My heart was beating hard. The dread of the early-morning phone call. I walked through the darkened house and checked the doors and windows. I tried to laugh aloud about the Creeper—what a silly, melodramatic name—but the house swallowed up the sound. Outside, the street was silent and deserted. Back in bed, the sheets smelled of Julie. Maybe around 5:00 A.M., I fell asleep.

I got downtown around 4:00 P.M. Peralta was on the phone when I reached his office, but he waved me in. I scanned the *Republic* on his desk: lots of crime news, but nothing about Phaedra or Greg Townsend. A few minutes later, he hung up.

His jaw clenched and unclenched as I told him about Julie.

"I'm going to get a warrant." He snatched up the phone.

"Mike, she was at work. It would have been a neat trick if she could have driven to Sedona, murdered Townsend—with a twelve-gauge shotgun, no less—and gotten back to work, but I don't see it."

He twirled the receiver in his massive hands. "Did you check?"

"No," I said. "I thought I was off the case, or 'never on it,' as you put it."

"Check," he said. Then, into the receiver: "Melinda, I want you to find Judge Garcia—I know he flew to Crested Butte to gamble this weekend—and draw up a warrant for him to sign on Julie Riding." He gave her the file number so she could find Julie's address and Social Security number. "If you don't hear from me in the next two hours, get the warrant signed and BOLO her. Murder one."

"Mike, I've been sleeping with her," I said.

"I know."

"That could lead to a mistrial."

"Maybe," he said. "Check. You're a sworn sheriff's deputy, whatever fucked-up personal history you have."

"And you like to fuck with people."

He barely—barely—cracked a smile.

"Do I get paid for doing this?" I asked.

"You get reimbursed with my goodwill," Peralta said. "And considering everything that's happened, you're probably going to need it."

"I talked to Harrison Wolfe yesterday."

Peralta sat up straight. "Wolfe?"

I told him what I knew. He listened through two caffeine-free diet Cokes and then pinched the bridge of his nose. "God, I need a drink and a cigar," he said.

We concealed our badges and ID cards and walked over to Tom's Tavern, which for half a century had been the meeting place of Arizona's political elite. I didn't even know it still existed. When we walked in, I was sweating nonstop. Peralta was immaculate in his cream-colored suit, bola tie, and summer Stetson. We made our way to the back through the cool semidarkness as Peralta worked the room: a congressman here, a superior court judge there. There was a caricature of him on a wall of famous people, riding a horse, aiming a six-gun. I was happy to be nobody. When we were settled, Peralta had a Kentucky premium bourbon on the rocks and I had a martini. He clipped and lighted a Churchill, luxuriously protected from politically correct conventions out in the broad world.

"This is an amazing place," Peralta said. "And here I am, just a poor kid from the barrio."

"Who studied at the Kennedy School at Harvard."

He took a languid drag on the cigar. "Why does he think she was killed by someone she knew?"

"He said the landlady found Rebecca's door opened, unlocked, and her luggage inside. He said if she disappeared that night, she would have had to open her door. Who was she likely to do that for? Someone she knew."

"Or somebody impersonating a cop."

I looked at him through the smoke and gloom. "Wolfe also said Rebecca's body didn't have the mutilations found on the other Creeper killings."

"That's thin," Peralta said.

"I think he's probably right."

"Why?" Peralta waved the cigar. "None of this was in the original reports."

"He said the county attorney took the reports."

"Oh Jesus," Peralta said. "Just another old cop trying to settle a score with his bosses."

"I believe him."

Peralta just looked at me like I was pathetic.

"Because he was the investigating officer," I went on. "He was there. Gut feelings count, too."

"Shit, here I am defending your work against you."

"I was sloppy, Mike. I moved too quickly on the research. I didn't do enough to verify what I found was true. It was methodology I wouldn't have allowed from an undergraduate. Cicero said the first law for a historian is that he shall never dare utter an untruth."

"Oh, who knows what truth is?" he said airily, mostly to get my goat, I think.

"Jesus, you sound like the tenure committee at San Diego State," I said, annoyed. "I think we need to look at the case further."

"You're obsessed." Peralta finished his bourbon and motioned for another. "You do it if you want, but it's gratis. And I have new work for you to do."

He knocked off an inch of fine ash and smiled a wolfish grin. "Tell me what the old son of a bitch was like."

Monday morning, I drove to the Phoenician. Julie's desk was empty when I walked into the marketing office. I asked to see the supervisor and was greeted by a pleasant-looking woman with high cheekbones and bobbed blond hair. She was wearing a trim gray suit. She introduced herself as Karen Dejulio, the director of sales. When I showed her my ID, she led me into a spacious private office overlooking the unreal green of the resort's vast golf course.

"Deputy Mapstone, is it?" She sat opposite me in front of the desk, crossing elegant legs. "A real-life western deputy."

I smiled and she went on. "I moved here last year from Michigan, and everything is still new and wonderful. My God, all the places to go rock climbing—I'm seriously into the lifestyle!"

I sunnily agreed, then asked about Julie Riding. First, she told me Julie was off today. Then, when I persisted, she told me it wasn't the Phoenician's policy to discuss personnel matters. I hated threatening beautiful women with search warrants, so I told her I had a mean boss—hell, that part was especially true—who wanted Julie for questioning in a case. Her smile went away, which was a loss. Then she closed the office door and came back. The elegant legs crossed again, this time the other way.

She sighed. "I wondered how long it would take for something like this to happen, Deputy Mapstone."

When I said nothing, she continued. "I mean, we've worked with Julie over and over. We have a very good employee assistance plan, and she's been referred to it twice. I suppose I was too indulgent."

"Why do you think I'm here, Ms. Dejulio?"

"Karen, please," she insisted. "Why, about Julie's cocaine habit, I assume. I mean, it's no secret, God knows. I just didn't think it would lead to the law getting involved. I mean, frankly, it's not as if a lot of the leading lights of Scottsdale don't like their nose candy. The back-to-basics nineties? Yeah, right."

I asked her if Julie had worked straight through the day Townsend was murdered.

"Yes, she was in at eight and stayed in the office all day," Karen said, "although she said she had to leave for a family emergency around four that day." I didn't exactly feel relieved. "We specifically worked on promptness and absenteeism with Julie during her last performance evaluation."

"You know her sister was found murdered that day?"

Karen Dejulio put her hand to her mouth and uttered a small gasp. "Oh, dear, I didn't even know she had a sister. That's horrible."

"Tell me about the cocaine," I said.

"Well, Julie had been here about six months when I took over, and it was obvious something was wrong. Her mood would change a lot. Some days her eyes just seemed rolled back in her head. And she was missing a lot of work. At first, I thought it was drinking, but then one day I caught her doing a line in the bathroom."

"Why didn't you fire her?"

"Well, she was very good when she was herself. I didn't want to lose her. And our lawyers felt we might be open to a lawsuit if she was found to be disabled by her addiction."

"But this was going on for at least the last year, right?"

"Deputy Mapstone, I think it was going on last week."

I left a business card with Karen Dejulio and asked her to call me if she heard from Julie. Then I walked out into the heat, feeling like a chump. What else had Julie lied to me about? Right that minute, in the harsh judgments the Arizona sun encourages, it felt like I had spent a lifetime being misled by Julie Riding. But it was hard to stay mad at her, not after all the pain she had confessed to me over the past several days. I just felt sad for her.

I got on the cellular phone and advised Peralta that she had been at work all day the day Townsend was killed. He ordered me to see him Wednesday for a new case. He and Sharon were going to fly over to San Diego tomorrow, he said. San Diego made me think of Patty and my mood got darker still. I shook my head and drove west.

When I pulled up at home, the front door was standing open. I jammed the Blazer into park, then pulled the Python from the glove compartment and unholstered it. I walked quickly to the side of the house and looked through a window. Inside, drawers were pulled out and shelves rummaged through. I couldn't see anybody. Insanely, I thought about the spike in the air conditioning bill the open door would cause. I cocked the Python and edged to the door.

I came through low and quick, then moved immediately behind the big leather chair. Nothing. Not a sound. There were papers and books all over. Somebody had given the place a real going-over, somebody with the balls to do it in the middle of the day no less. I made it room by room, checking under the bed, in the closets, behind the shower curtain. I was breathing very hard for no reason. I uncocked the revolver and walked to the front door to close it. The lock had been picked, not broken. It relatched itself with no problem. But whoever had been there didn't want to conceal the fact.

I dropped into the big chair and surveyed the mess. My family's home, violated. For what? This was no burglary—the valuables, such as they were, were all still here. Someone had been looking for something.

The phone made me jump.

"You're still looking where you're not supposed to look," came a man's voice. It was the voice from the carport, measured and detached.

"Who is this?" I asked stupidly.

"You're all alone in the world, Mapstone. No wife or family. No real job. Nobody'd miss you if you just disappeared into the desert. Leave it alone."

"Looking into what?" I demanded, but he had already hung up. And in my head, I could hear Julie's strange trill, hear her saying, "I think we're in great danger."

I was watering the hedges and palm trees the next morning, thinking how for the first time in my life Julie Riding had said she loved me, when an old Honda Prelude pulled up. My first jumpy thought was that the gun was inside the house. But out stepped Lindsey, looking very cool in a cotton print skirt and carrying a bag and some files. She called out, "Hey, History Shamus," and we went in out of the heat.

"I have the day off, and thought you might like a bagel," she said, then, surveying the living room, added, "You're kinda messy, Dave, not to be judgmental or anything. It just seems at odds with that orderly Virgo mind of yours."

"Somebody paid me a visit yesterday, looking for something. They went through every drawer and cabinet and closet, even looked under mattresses and in the crawl space of the attic. I've also learned the Rebecca Stokes case is still wide open."

She took my hand and led me into the kitchen, where she pulled out bottles of champagne and orange juice. "You put the nova lox spread on the bagels, and I'll make mimosas," she said. "Where were your case files?"

"Safe. I had my briefcase and PowerBook in the Blazer."

Lindsey tossed her dark hair a little and popped the cork. "You are jumpy, Dave," she said, putting a hand on my wrist. I told her about the conversation with Julie and the warning phone call—and the encounter in the carport a few weeks ago.

"Cheers," she said, handing me a mimosa. "You've landed in some bad shit somehow. Who is this Julie?"

"We went together back in college."

"Did you, like, disco dance and wear platform shoes?"

She made me smile. "I didn't hear from her for twenty years. Then she turns up on my doorstep a few weeks ago, asking me to find her sister."

"Phaedra? I read your report. How did Julie even know you were back in the city?"

"She ran into Peralta one day, and he told her. My bad luck." I explained about Julie and the cocaine, the behavior swings and now the disappearance.

Lindsey sat demurely on the butcher-block table and sipped thoughtfully, the bubbles tickling her nose. "Dames is trouble, History Shamus," she said in a lower voice.

"I've been doing some checking on my own into some things," she went on. "I started running this Greg Townsend through some databases, and, surprise, there's a DEA file on him."

"You can get into the DEA?"

She cocked an eyebrow. "Confidential informants say he was flying in drugs from Mexico for Bobby Hamid."

"Julie said he had his own plane," I said. "Tell me about this Bobby Hamid."

"Whoa, Dave, you have been gone from Phoenix for a while. Let me see, Ruhollah Hamid, son of a wealthy Iranian family, came here to study at Arizona State; then the revolution changed things and he stayed. Opened a Dunkin' Donuts franchise with family money, did reasonably well. Then he opened a topless club. But in the late 1980s, intelligence reports start linking him to drug running, mostly small shit back then. But over five years or so, he becomes a real player: drugs, prostitution, guns. He has some major alliances with the Crips to run methamphetamines, the Mexican Mafia for heroin. Some people believe Bobby Hamid is the godfather now."

"Jeez," I said. "You miss a little, you miss a lot. Has he done time?"

"He's been arrested about a dozen times—he's one of Chief Peralta's pet obsessions—but no convictions. Can't find anybody to narc on him. He keeps his distance from the operating side of the business. He's also got three fast-food franchises that are totally legitimate; he gives away lots of money, even serves on boards and charities. Whenever he gets busted, he claims he's a victim of anti-Iranian prejudice."

"Lindsey, how do you keep all this in your head?"

"Same way you do, Dave. We're both weird. By the way, do you know what Julie's married name was? I want to run her." I gave it to her.

"Understand about Bobby Hamid: He wears two-thousand-dollar suits and has a pretty blond beach bunny wife, but he's a killer. He wouldn't have risen this fast without being one."

"And Townsend was flying for him?" I asked.

"Apparently. You know these CI reports can be unreliable. But when he ends up dead, that gives it credence. Bobby Hamid would have a guy shotgunned in his bed, five rounds of double-ought buckshot, including one in the mouth. That's his style."

"So if Townsend got on the wrong side of this guy, maybe Phaedra did, too. And that's what Julie knows but never told me."

Lindsey bit her lip thoughtfully. "Maybe. Maybe, but it doesn't quite add up. Phaedra looks like she was quite a beautiful girl. If she pissed off Bobby, he would have just sold her into slavery."

She saw my look.

"Oh, yeah, there's quite a market in the Middle East and Asia for pretty young American redheads. A sheik or the boss of a drug cartel would have paid thousands of dollars for her. And we strongly suspect Bobby has been behind some of that."

My stomach felt very cold. "Don't be squeamish, Dave. It's the new millennium. This is the world we're left with." She gave me that sardonic smile. "God is dead, remember?"

"Another thing people kept telling me was that Phaedra hated drugs," I said. "So it doesn't add up, if I was being told the truth, which would be a first."

"Oh, poor Dave," Lindsey said, teasing me. "He's back with the cops, and everybody lies to him."

"So that leaves us—where?" I asked. "Is Bobby Hamid the one behind these threats or not?"

"If he's not, he'd probably know who is," Lindsey said. "What, are you going to walk in and ask him?"

"I might want a couple of chocolate doughnuts." I smiled.

"Be very careful, Dave. I think the city has changed a lot more than you realize. But for your professional perusal . . ." She handed me a sheaf of files on Townsend and Bobby Hamid.

"Now," she said, "tell me about the Stokes case still being open."

John Rogers was dozing in his hospital bed when we walked up, but he quickly roused himself and took Lindsey in.

"The deputies look a hell of a lot better than when I used to see 'em," he muttered. I guess I was surprised he remembered me. He was still looking Lindsey over. "What the hell's that gold thing in your nose?"

"This is Deputy Adams," I said.

"Lindsey."

"Sit, sit." The big man waved his hands. "They told me yesterday this cancer in my prostate has gone too far. Sorry, miss. Anyway, they tell me there's nothing they can do that won't just kill me outright. I say, just keep me from the damned pain."

"I'm sorry, John. I didn't even realize—"

He shook his head. "Doesn't matter. Wish I could see my son and daughter. Wish we hadn't all gotten so far away from the old ways. Never mattered to me when I was younger. Hell, it's all over. Red folks, white folks, black folks. The whole goddamned thing is falling apart."

"John, we hate to bother you, but we had some more questions about the Creeper cases."

"I saw the newspaper. You did okay."

"I talked to Harrison Wolfe."

John Rogers visibly stiffened. "My God, Mr. Wolfe is still alive?" I nodded. "I always wondered if he was really human."

"What do you mean?"

"Ah, don't matter. Mr. Wolfe always respected Indians. He was a friend of mine, as much as anybody ever was his friend."

"He said the women killed by the Creeper were mutilated. True?"

Rogers looked at Lindsey and back at me. He nodded slowly.

"But Rebecca Stokes wasn't?"

"As I remember it, she wasn't. It wasn't my call, but you know how the guys talk about cases."

"So her murder wasn't related?"

He sighed and splayed his big hands.

"Cops always talk, Officer Rogers," Lindsey said softly. "What did you guys think?"

Rogers smiled a toothless smile at her. "My first sergeant said, 'You ain't paid to think here, chief.' Let me put it to you this way. It was an embarrassment to the Phoenix Police that the Stokes case was never solved. But we wasn't exactly beating the bushes. All my snitches on the street were totally dry. There was no talk about it on the street."

"Wolfe said her luggage was found inside the apartment door. So she wasn't snatched between the taxi and the front door, even though that's what had always assumed."

"Don't know that."

"Wolfe said the county attorney took the reports."

Rogers stared at me a long time, his eyelids steadily drooping. "You're a smart fella," he said finally. "Why would that happen?"

"Because she was the governor's niece," Lindsey observed, "and they were hiding something."

Rogers snored softly and we watched him for a while, hoping for more, knowing we wouldn't get it. We walked out quietly, and I told Lindsey about a surviving witness to Rebecca's life.

* * *

Opal Harvey insisted on getting us iced tea and cookies. We waited in the cool dimness of the living room as Lindsey picked at the doilies on the furniture arms and looked at me with one eyebrow raised. "Frozen in 1930 middle-class earnestness," she said softly. "Kill me if I ever do this."

"I promise," I said.

"I sent a copy of the newspaper to my granddaughter," came the mechanical voice. "I said, 'I was part of that.' "

"I appreciate your help, Mrs. Harvey. There's just some loose ends we're tying up."

I led off half a dozen times with questions about Rebecca's habits, family, friends. About the neighborhood. About the Creeper. Nothing.

Finally, Lindsey asked, "I bet she was pretty lonely, Rebecca. Living so far from home. Only twenty-one years old. Back then, everybody was supposed to be married by that age."

Opal Harvey started to put the wand to her voice box and then stopped, looking out the blinds for long minutes. "Oh, honey," she finally said. "Rebecca had a lover."

She sipped some tea and went on slowly. "I've never told anyone that. I didn't want to hurt the family. I didn't want anyone to think she was cheap, because she wasn't. She was a good girl. . . ." The thought trailed off.

"Who was he, Mrs. Harvey?" Lindsey asked.

"I never knew." She studied her hands. "Rebecca kept him a secret and I never intruded on that. I think he was married, because he only came at night, and he never stayed with her. It was still a small town back then, and people would have talked. I know this: He was older. He dressed well and drove a nice car. I always wished he would have picked her up at the train station that night—I guess I assumed he would, since Rebecca said she didn't need a ride from us."

"Did you ever see him again after she disappeared?"

Opal Harvey shook her head.

Afterward, out in Lindsey's Prelude, waiting for the air-conditioning to cool things down, I felt the rush of discovery, however slight. But

Lindsey was quiet, her eyes unreadable. "Most murder victims knew their murderers," she said.

"The lover?" I said. She nodded.

"But we know she was picked up at Union Station that night by a taxi. The driver was a moonlighting Phoenix policeman."

"Maybe the lover was waiting for her at home. Maybe she went to him."

"Motive?"

"Who needs a motive when you're in love?" Lindsey said.

I should have gone to see Peralta Wednesday morning. Instead, I called his secretary to put off our meeting. She said he had been called to a meeting with the county supervisors and was in a very bad mood. "So it's probably just as well," she said. Just as well: She didn't know the half of it.

The morning paper had news of a gunfight between rival gangs in Maryvale, which once upon a time not so long ago was a neighborhood synonymous with suburban safety and blandness. And there was the obituary of the veteran TV anchorman who had read the evening news when I was growing up. My grandparents would let me watch the ten o'clock news, and this man with a blond pompadour and black plastic glasses had been a figure of reassurance, a bookend on the days. He had been retired for years, of course. But I had been away. Little by little, everything in my past in this city was passing.

I tried to act normal. I went over to Phoenix College and lectured to my students in the survey course on the origins of the Civil War. Faces—hot, eager, bored, distracted. Most of the younger students were hearing this for the first time, so rotten is the teaching of history in high schools. Once, that would have motivated me or depressed me, but that day I just wanted to get through it. Slavery, states' rights, the passing of the compromisers from the scene. "John Brown's body lies a-mouldering in the grave." I kept seeing the faces of Rebecca Stokes and Phaedra Riding. I am the keeper of murdered souls.

All I had wanted was a summer at home to get my bearings and some easy work from Mike Peralta. Instead, I was in the middle of—what? Three unsolved murders. Two warnings to quit looking into something. Thoughts of Lindsey—too many thoughts. Too many questions. You wouldn't think anxiety and paranoia would grow so much in a city of endless sunny days, tanned goddesses, and opulent resorts. You would be wrong. It was a concrete desert and this was high summer.

I went to a gun shop and bought two sets of speed loaders for the Python and three boxes of rounds heavy enough to drop a gorilla. I wore extra-extra-large shirts, attempting, with little success, to conceal the bulk of the gun on my hip. So I just started clipping my star on my belt all the time and carrying openly.

I finished cleaning up the mess at home. After work, Lindsey came over and we drank Bloody Marys and listened to Billy Strayhorn and Charlie Parker CDs. It would have seemed reassuring if I hadn't felt the constant heavy tug of the Colt Python on my belt. Lindsey carried a baby Glock 9-mm automatic in her purse, nine rounds compactly held in the magazine, "ready to rock 'n' roll," as she put it.

That night, we sat out in the garden and defied the heat, listening to the cicadas and the city noise. We swapped life stories. I learned that she was a another Virgo, born twenty-seven years before—"on Labor Day," she deadpanned.

She was an Air Force brat. She came to the Valley when she was three, when her dad was stationed at Williams Air Force Base. Her middle name was Faith. "Hey, it was the seventies," she said.

After high school, she tried college but was bored. "No offense," she said. Hell, I'd been bored with it, too. So she enlisted and went into the Air Police. After four years, she knew she hated being told what to do, so she came home and tried college again. "Still boring." She went to work for the Sheriff's Office. That was five years ago. She'd been fooling with computers since she was fourteen. No training, but, she said, "I know how computers think." There was an unhappy love affair with a lawyer named John. She lived in Sunnyslope with a cat.

She stretched her legs out onto my lap and I massaged her feet, nice feet with long, athletic ankles and delicate toes. I told her more about my life.

I gave her the short version: I am a Phoenix native born at Good Samaritan Hospital. An only child. My parents were killed in a plane crash. Little kids play that "orphan game" when they get mad at their folks. But it was real for me. My mom's parents raised me. Grandfather was a dentist, named Philip—I carried that as my middle name. Grandmother sold real estate; her name was Ella. It was a good childhood. In college, I thought I'd be a lawyer and save the world. But I didn't like the idea of defending bad guys, and I didn't want to stay in school forever. So I got my B.A. and went to the Sheriff's Academy. When I knew I didn't want to be a cop, I went back to college part-time, studied history, and grew to love it. So I got my Ph.D. and, in those ironies life springs on us, stayed in school, teaching in Ohio and California. Got married. Got divorced. No kids. It all sounded neater than it was.

When I was done, she asked, "Why are you attracted to emotionally unavailable women?"

"I didn't see it that way at the time. I saw brilliant, creative women who had suffered and wanted so desperately to be loved."

"Maybe I'm emotionally unavailable," Lindsey said.

I said, "Maybe I am, too."

I got back from class a little after 2:00 P.M. Thursday and the phone was ringing. I expected it might be the Realtor I had called about listing the house, but it was a woman's voice.

"We've met," she said. "We met in an apartment a couple of weeks ago. But please don't say my name."

"Okay."

"I need very much to talk to you. There are some important things you don't know."

"Are you—"

"Be careful, Dr. Mapstone. If you know what I mean."

I did. "How should we proceed?" I asked.

"Go to the place where you get your messages when you're working," she said. "I'll be in touch."

I had to think about it for a minute, but then I remembered that I had a mailbox in the Social Sciences Department at Phoenix College. I drove back up Nineteenth Avenue and got there between classes. In the box, aside from two weeks' worth of mindless administrative drivel, I found an envelope with my name on it, and inside that a folded sheet of stationery with the message: "Metrocenter. Ruby Tuesday, 8:30 tonight."

I tucked it in my pocket and wondered why Susan Knightly wanted to talk to me.

Back at home, the answering machine was empty. I picked up the phone and called Lorie Pope at the *Republic*. It had only been about two years since we'd spoken.

"Lorie, it's David Mapstone."

"David," she said. "My God, what a surprise. I read about you and was going to call."

"I guess I should ask if you're on deadline?"

"No," she said. "But thanks for asking."

"Remember when I helped you with that Latin American history paper senior year?"

"You saved my life, David. Of course I remember."

"Well, I'm callin' in favors. How about lunch tomorrow?"

"I'm intrigued," she said. "Okay. Come by the newsroom around eleven-forty-five, and then we'll go somewhere."

I needed the comfort of books, so I drove over to the public library and took the glass elevator up to the Arizona Collection. The building—popularly dubbed the "copper toaster" because of its abstract design—was nearly new, with an atrium pool that you would walk into if you weren't careful and a stunning view of the skyscrapers of the central corridor—as if you were suspended above the year-round green of palm trees and oleanders and the concrete and glass monuments that marched north and south between the mountains.

An indulgent librarian pulled me the papers of John Henry McConnico, twelfth governor of Arizona, as well as a couple of Ph.D. dissertations on microfiche from the U of A on the McConnico years in Arizona. I popped open the PowerBook and set up some files: names, chronology, family history, things to check later. I picked through the dusty books and started making notes. And then I asked for something else: a small history of the Phoenix Police Department, written in 1965 by a former professor of mine. I didn't really know what I was looking for, but perhaps something would get me moving again on Rebecca Stokes—or maybe give me the inspiration to start writing another history book I couldn't finish.

A little after 8:00 P.M., I pulled into the vast parking lot of Metrocenter, Jim Morrison on the radio singing "L.A. Woman." City at night. Arizona doesn't go on daylight saving time, partly out of libertarian cussedness and partly because if it did, the sun would still be out at 10:00 P.M., a source of misery nobody on the political spectrum wanted to contemplate. So the sun was gone, but the heat remained god-awful. The mall was something like the biggest in the world when it opened, on the outskirts of Phoenix, in the mid-1970s. Most people back then couldn't figure why they built it so far out. But now, of course, the Metrocenter was deep inside the city and even starting to show its age. I found a parking spot within a hundred yards of the entrance to the food court and walked slowly toward the doors, watching cars and people.

Inside, it was cool, bright, and crowded. Phoenix nearly invented the indoor shopping mall and had elevated it to something like a lifestyle. So here on a Thursday night, away from the empty sidewalks and parks, was humanity's ocean, retail-style. I wound my way through the food court, past families with twofer prams and saw teenage girl mall rats, full grown on the outside, wearing the briefest short-shorts and deep in conversation with one another. I found refuge in Ruby Tuesday, and waited by the bar.

At 8:45, a woman in black jeans and a linen shirt leaned on the rail beside me.

"I'm sorry for the cloak-and-dagger routine," she said. "But I think you'll agree it's justified."

It was Susan Knightly. She looked very different from the well-coiffed Susan I had first met. Her shoulder-length strawberry blond hair was concealed under a black Nikon ball cap. We went to a back booth of the bar. I could imagine the calls Peralta would get for me being in a bar with my badge hanging from my belt. I ordered a martini anyway. She ordered a chardonnay.

"You know about Phaedra?" I asked. She nodded. "I'm sorry I didn't call you."

"I assumed you were busy," she said. "Let me get right to the point, Dr. Mapstone, or is it Deputy Mapstone?"

"How about David?"

"David." She gave a small smile. "I don't trust the police in this matter. I don't really know why I am trusting you, but I guess I've got to trust someone, or else go on living this way."

"Why don't you trust the police?"

"Phaedra told me not to," she said.

"When did she tell you this?" I asked.

"Two weeks ago."

Susan looked at me straight on with those green eyes. Her face was a scrimshaw of freckles and soft laugh lines.

"Phaedra wasn't kidnapped," she said. "She was on the run."

I felt another kick in the stomach.

"I am getting so tired of being lied to."

"I couldn't tell you," Susan said. "I promised her. God, I wanted to go to the police every day, but Phaedra made me swear I wouldn't. And the more that happened, the more I got paranoid."

"So when you found me in her apartment . . ."

"I was getting her some clothes."

"I might have been able to help her."

"Do you think I haven't thought of that?" Susan said in a low, desolate voice, and her eyes filled with tears.

She looked around the room—tan young men and women clustered close to the bar, lost in an unintelligible jabber—and leaned close to me. "One night in June, it was the twentieth, I got home and got a call from Phaedra. She said someone was trying to kill her, and that she couldn't work for me anymore. That was all she would tell me then. But she called back in a couple of days, and I made her let me give her some clothes and money.

"That's where I got her apartment key, so I could get her some clothes, look after her stuff. Although, God knows, I realize in retrospect that it was foolish of me to go to her apartment. At the time, I guess we figured they were looking for her, and that nobody would think anything about me going to the apartment complex."

"You better hope they're able to discriminate between their redheads," I said. "Who is 'they,' by the way?"

"I'm not exactly sure," Susan said. "It was a dope deal gone wrong. Phaedra's boyfriend was a pilot who did dope runs from Mexico. He just decided to take a shipment, I guess. Rip off his client. Phaedra got caught in the middle of it."

"Bobby Hamid?" I asked.

"I didn't hear that name."

"Who, then?"

"She wouldn't say. She said she overheard things she wasn't supposed to hear, so they wanted to kill her. She was afraid to tell me too much. She did say they had paid off DEA and the cops, and that if she went to the police, she was as good as dead."

"So she hid out for a month?"

Susan nodded. "She crashed with friends here and there. She never wanted to stay anywhere long; she felt she might be endangering her friends. Sometimes she was afraid she was being followed."

"What about her sister or her mother?"

"I don't know." Susan shook her head. "She said she didn't know whom to trust. She didn't want to talk about her sister. It always upset her."

"And you believed her?"

"I've been followed," Susan said. "I had my studio broken into last week, but nothing was taken. Probably two hundred and fifty thousand dollars in cameras, computers, and equipment—and nothing taken. Just files rifled, that kind of thing. A couple of threatening phone calls, said I needed to mind my own business."

"So what happened to Phaedra? Whoever was after her just caught up?"

"I don't know." She silently drummed slender freckled fingers on the bar. "The last time I talked to Phaedra was a week ago Monday. There was something she wasn't telling me. She was very agitated. I offered to give her a thousand dollars so she could get out of the state, and she agreed. We were going to meet the next night, here. But she never showed up. Then I read about it in the *Republic* two days later."

I asked her if she would go downtown and give a statement. I guaranteed she would be safe.

"I'll think about it," she said, and rose to go.

"Susan." I stood. "If you're in danger, let me help you."

She looked back at me and adjusted the ball cap. "I'm good at taking care of myself, David. I'm not sure I'm ready to trust anybody else just yet. I'll call you tomorrow."

I followed her out of the tavern into the brightness of the mall atrium. The kids were mostly gone, replaced by couples and clusters of young women in black miniskirts and men in tight jeans coming and going from the movie theater. Susan looked around the crowd, then walked over to the railing and surveyed the lower levels of the mall. Turning back to me, she said, "You have brothers and sisters, David?"

I said I didn't.

"Hmm." She thought about that. "Then you wouldn't appreciate what—"

That second, I heard a woman scream and caught a flash of blue metal out of the corner of my eye. Susan's eyes grew gigantic and she dropped to the floor as the glass wall behind her blew out. I felt shards of glass in my neck and face as I fell sideways and rolled. People flashed by, yelling and screaming.

I scanned the crowd and saw a muscular man—he couldn't have been taller than five five—with dark hair, tank top, and a machine gun with a large silencer aimed at me. Julie had talked of a small muscular man following her. I grabbed for the Python as I saw a muzzle flash and heard an odd *whack-whack-whack* sound. Bullets ricocheted off the polished metal railings. The revolver slid out of its nylon holster, resting heavily in my hand.

"Down!" I said. "Get down!" People stared dumbly at me. "Police officer!" I rose slowly, the gun held in both hands, quickly scanning for the small muscular man. I caught sight of him maybe twenty-five feet away. He looked at me coolly and raised the machine gun. I couldn't get a shot—too many people. "Get down on the floor, goddamn it!" I shouted, then aimed and pulled back, aimed again, no clean shot. "Down!" He had me. Shit.

But nothing happened.

He cursed and slapped the gun. A jam.

He turned and ran into the mall. I started after him.

"Stay here!" I commanded Susan Knightly, who was still on the floor. To an ashen-faced man crouched against a bench, I said, "Call nine one one."

"Tell them a plainclothes officer is on the scene and in pursuit of a suspect." Hopefully, the cops wouldn't mistakenly shoot me.

"Hey, need some help?" A burly red-faced man showed me a revolver in his belt. I nearly shot him just out of reflex.

"No!" I said. "Put that thing away! Do not follow me!"

I ran after the small man. It was pure adrenaline. Past the atrium and the bars, the mall immediately became deserted. I could hear Peralta from eighteen years ago telling me to calm down, that calmness meant steady judgment—and a good aim. I ran past the glassed and gated stores, watching the guy tear down an escalator. Reaching the top, I proceeded cautiously, waiting for a burst of fire—but he was gone. I padded down the escalator in a crouch, the Python in a two-handed combat grip, my hands only shaking a little. I was alone on the lower level and caught my breath. My cheek was bleeding steadily now from the glass. He could have gone in any of a half dozen directions.

This is nuts, a voice in my head warned. Wait for the cops.

Except that he knew why Susan Knightly and I were targets.

I picked a direction and ran that way, hugging close to a wall, ready to meet my killer around every post or alcove. I went a hundred feet and stopped, listening. I could still hear screaming and shouting from the bar area. Maybe some sirens in the distance. A fan whining somewhere. Empty storefronts and mannequins. A fountain's rush. My own breathing. A burning in my lungs.

Footsteps.

He bolted suddenly from a doorway, turned down an exit corridor, his steps echoing behind him.

"Deputy sheriff! Stop!" I yelled, close behind him now. "Stop!"

I raised the revolver and lined up the Colt's twin sights. Right between the shoulder blades: Bye-bye, asshole.

I didn't take the shot. He banged out the fire exit into the night.

I ran after him and had just reached the exit bar when a voice stopped me from behind.

"Drop your weapon! Drop your weapon! Do not move!"

I heard the chilling sound of a round being chambered in a semiautomatic pistol.

I froze. "I'm a deputy sheriff," I called, still facing toward the exit door. I let the Python down easy. "The suspect just ran outside here."

"Mister, I don't know who the hell you are," came a scared young voice. "But I want you facedown on the ground, hands spread straight out! Push your weapon away very slowly!"

"Let me show you my ID."

"Mister, you are five seconds away from eternity."

A big drop of sweat trickled down my spine. Or maybe it was blood.

I almost started to turn around and yell that the son of a bitch was getting away. But I thought better of it. I got facedown on the cold, dirty mall floor and pushed the Python gently away.

I sat in the back of a large, bright fire department ambulance as a fireman in a dark blue T-shirt picked glass out of my neck and cheek. It stung like hell. But the good news was that I was the only casualty of the gunfire. The air-conditioning was running, but I was sweating nonstop. Peralta—wearing a tux—and three Phoenix cops surrounded me, firing questions.

"What direction did he go in after exiting the mall?"

"What vehicle did he drive?"

"Did he have anyone else with him in the parking lot?"

"Ow." I winced. "I've told you five times, I never got out the door after him because the officer behind me wouldn't let me go."

"He didn't know who you were," said a uniformed police captain who had a tuft of hair missing from his cop mustache.

"I tried to tell him," I said.

"How do you know you and this unknown woman were the intended targets?" asked a Phoenix PD deputy chief, a slim, bloodless man wearing a gray herringbone suit that was wildly out of place in the heat. "Dressing like an easterner," my grandfather would have called it.

"Well, he looked at me, chambered a round, and pointed the

gun. And the first burst came right at the woman who was giving me information on a homicide case."

"I don't know," the captain said skeptically.

"Mike, Susan Knightly was in touch with Phaedra just before she died." Peralta raised his eyebrows, and I related Susan's conversation. Then I told him about the break-in at my house—and the beating I'd gotten in the carport. He asked a couple of questions and made some notes. He handed back my Python.

The Phoenix cops weren't impressed.

"What were you doing at the mall, Mapstone?" This from a slender detective in a Ralph Lauren shirt with sweat rings under the arms.

"I was going to the twelve-hour sale at Dillard's," I said. "How many times do we have to go over this? Are you out looking for the shooter? Where is Susan, Mike?"

He shook his head. "She was gone when the first units arrived."

"Jesus."

The fireman soaked my neck with Betadine. The gauze pads looked as if I were bleeding rusty radiator water.

"If there was a Susan," said the deputy chief.

Peralta said, "Fuck you, Frank. I don't question the motives of your officers."

"My officers, Mike," the deputy chief said, seething, "don't get into shoot-outs involving submachine guns at crowded malls in the county's jurisdiction."

"If I can't get a city APB on this woman," Peralta said, "I'll just get Chief Wilson out of bed to discuss the matter. We were supposed to meet for golf first thing in the morning, but I'll be happy to wake him now."

The deputy chief looked long and hard at Peralta. "Okay," he said. "You are a real prick, Peralta."

"But I'm not a city prick."

"This guy's not even a real deputy," protested Ralph Lauren. He went on talking as if I were one of the IV poles on the stretcher: "I'm still not convinced this shooter wasn't some disgruntled employee at Metrocenter, or maybe he was pissed because his wife was at one of those nightspots with another man."

"Hello," I said to nobody in particular. "Did IQs fall dramatically among city cops during the years I was gone from law enforcement?"

Three pairs of eyes squinted at me.

"The point, gentlemen, is that this woman came forward to give new information on the murder of Phaedra Riding." I faced Ralph Lauren and spoke very slowly, "Mur-der, murder.

"Somebody was trying to keep Susan Knightly from talking. And he damned near succeeded. She said she didn't trust the cops in this case, and this won't exactly bolster her confidence. The thing we'd better be thinking is that somebody was willing to blow away damn near a whole shopping mall full of people to keep her from talking to us." I looked at Ralph again. "I'm sorry, Detective. Talking to *me.*"

Afterward, Peralta walked me back to the Blazer, both of us bathed in the blue-and-red wash of emergency lights and the harsh whiteness of TV cameras kept at a distance.

"You okay?" Peralta asked.

"I suppose," I said. "It's been a few years since somebody pointed a gun at me."

"Why didn't you tell me about this assault in your carport?"

"I guess I was ashamed," I said. "You were my self-defense instructor, remember?"

Peralta grunted, pulled a cigar from his tux, then smelled it and clipped it. He slowly shook his head and said, "What the hell have you gotten yourself into, Mapstone?"

We walked on, and he lit the cigar until the end flamed.

"Now do you believe me about Phaedra not being connected to the Harquahala murders?"

The cigar tip glowed. "I don't know what I believe," Peralta said. "I think we need to let the task force detectives do their job."

My head ached. "God, you are a stubborn SOB."

"Look, David, I'm feeling some heat here. The FBI's gotten involved in these serial killings. The county attorney's going crazy. It's only a matter of time before the media blow this thing out. I hear what you're saying about Phaedra and the drug angle, but she was also found in the vicinity of the other Harquahala victims. How do you know she didn't just answer the wrong personal ad?"

I sighed and unlocked the Blazer door. "How was San Diego?"

"Sharon wants to buy a condo facing the bay," he said glumly. "We're never going to get out of debt."

Gen. Omar Bradley did algebra problems to relax. I was never any good at math, so I drove. East on Dunlap into Sunnyslope. Count Basie in the CD player. Why had I never learned to do anything useful, like play jazz piano? South on Seventh Avenue, past sleeping neighborhoods of large, well-landscaped houses. The guy on the phone was right: Nobody would miss me. Hell, the cops didn't even believe me. Left turn on Glendale Avenue, through the thinning traffic of a late Thursday night. Eyes checking the rearview mirror more than usual. Did he follow Susan to the mall? Or did he follow me?

Across the Arizona Canal and up Lincoln Drive into the foothills of Paradise Valley. The lights gave way a bit as the city neighborhoods were replaced by acre lots and privacy walls. A black Saab whisked past me at eighty and disappeared into the distance. My stomach reflexively tightened. Phaedra landed in the middle of a drug rip-off. By Greg Townsend? So they kill them both? It had the terrible thoroughness of drug-related homicides. South on Tatum Boulevard, saguaro cactus and palm trees flashing in the headlights. Basie cooking. Camelback Mountain looming gigantic, straight ahead, a necklace of lights around its base that predated the prohibition on building on the mountains.

Except—why was Greg Townsend so calm when I showed up at his house? Why was he even at his house if he had ripped off a dope dealer and was hiding out? And why did he call me in the first place? Could it be as simple as Peralta was hinting? That Phaedra ended up in the wrong place at the wrong time—with the wrong man? Just like we thought about Rebecca Stokes. No, no.

I made a U-turn and headed back to Lincoln, then took Twenty-fourth Street back toward downtown. I needed *the view* and it didn't disappoint me: a vast sea of lights stretching west and south to the horizon. Off in the distance, the dark form of South Mountain and the Estrellas contained the brightness. TV towers on the South Mountains blinked red. City of American refugees, fast money and fresh starts. City of uneasy memories. City of lost sisters. My city.

Phaedra. She wasn't murdered with shotgun blasts or a Colombian necktie or any of the usual gruesome killing methods of the drug world. She was killed in a way that resembled a high-profile murder from forty years before, which had recently been in the newspapers again—a story involving a certain unemployed history professor turned deputy sheriff. None of it made sense.

I dropped back down into the city neighborhoods below Camelback Road, heading south on Twenty-fourth Street, thinking about what the detective had said. No, I wasn't a real deputy. But I had never been a "real" anything. When all my little friends had siblings to fight with, I was an only child. Later, when they played student radicals, I became a deputy. I was too left-wing for the cops and too right-wing for the ivory tower. When the sexual revolution was at its peak, I couldn't get a date. I could never stop thinking and just go along with the crowd. I could never fit that one-dimensional, sound-bite mold of late-twentieth-century man. In a postliterate society, I read books. In an age of moral relativism, I chased after things like truth and honor. As people obsessed about their health, I enjoyed Mexican food and liquor and good cigars. When Mike Peralta told me to keep out of a murder case, I remained mired in it.

Predestination or free will? A fellow named Erasmus couldn't settle the issue, so I wouldn't even try. Basie might have known the right answer, lodged somewhere in that tight congress of piano and brass and drums.

I drove through the empty streets of downtown, past skyscrapers lighted only for the janitors. Past the new baseball stadium and the new science museum. The America West Arena preened glamorously on the corner of Jefferson and Third Street, THE SHOWPLACE OF THE SOUTHWEST, a massive electric sign proclaimed to a deserted street. Basketball season was over, and it had been a bad one for the Suns.

I turned down Fourth Avenue and drove past the charming Spanish mission–style Union Station, which sat dark and abandoned. Rebecca Stokes had stepped off a train here in 1959, when the building was the center of the city's life. I could imagine the stainless-steel passenger cars and the rush of people under the lamps of the station platform. Catch a cab home and . . .

"What happened to you, Rebecca?" I asked aloud. "Whom did you go meet? You must have been thinking about him as the train pulled in."

Now the trains were gone from Union Station. Nobody home. All alone in the desert. All alone in the world. I thought momentarily of Patty. Two Phoenix PD units sat across from the new City Hall, distracted by a traffic stop, happily unaware of me. I had come within a heartbeat, a moment's judgment, of killing a man tonight. I had come within a mechanical malfunction of being dead myself. Basie was done. I continued north in silence, over the underground freeway, past my old grade school, slowly driving toward home. The rearview mirror was dark and empty.

The newsroom of the *Arizona Republic,* on the ninth floor of the paper's brand-new downtown tower, looked more like an insurance company office than a scene out of *The Front Page.* No stogie-chomping city editor. No screaming eccentrics in green eyeshades. No clattering typewriters, jangling phones, or reporters in fedoras yelling, "Get me rewrite, sweetheart." Just decorator-driven corporate blandness against picture-window views of the mountains. The subdued background sound of computer keystrokes was the only noise. Men in beards and women in sensible shoes walked briskly past me with notebooks in their hands and sour looks on their faces. I gave my name to a receptionist who looked about twelve years old and waited for Lorie Pope.

The first time I saw her was on a murder scene in 1980, when I was a green deputy standing watch out in the heat and she was a young reporter intern, just arrived from Jersey, who couldn't get past the police line. Maybe we were both rookies kept on the outside and maybe she just took pity on me, but, with eighties female assertiveness, she asked for my phone number. I was on the rebound from Julie, so Lorie and I ended up dating for a few months. After that, we remained friends, and after I moved away, I tried to look her up when I came back to visit. I knew she'd been in and out of two marriages, converted in turn to est, Buddhism, and Judaism, and wrote an award-winning book on organized crime (I even got a brief mention in the acknowledgements). She left Arizona to work at newspapers in Seattle and L.A., then came back to the *Republic* as the head of its investigations team.

"David! My God!"

We hugged, a long, genuine hug. Lorie Pope was lean, tall, and tan, with dark hair cut fashionably short. Although she had changed over the years—grown into her face, is that the expression?—she looked at least ten years younger than I knew she was. And her laugh was just as I remembered it: uninhibited, infectious, wonderful.

She patted the holster on my belt. "Things have gotten tougher in the classroom, no?"

"I could have used it there, actually." I laughed, and she led me out of the building, walking her brisk, purposeful walk.

"You're quite the hero," she said. "Uncovering information about a forty-year-old murder case, and one involving a relative of the next governor no less."

"Is that the prediction for Brent McConnico?" I asked.

"If not this next election, then the one after."

"He took me to lunch," I said. "Seemed nice enough, for a politician."

"I think he's slimy," Lorie said.

The heat of the sidewalk was burning my feet. I asked her why she didn't like McConnico.

"When you want an afternoon's primer on Arizona politics, and if you're making the martinis, I'll tell you. For one thing, he's married and he's tried on more than one occasion to pick me up."

Five minutes through the midday hell and we were in a cool, dark booth in a restaurant at Arizona Center. She ordered a Bloody Mary. Wearing badge and gun, I settled for a diet Coke.

"So you're really back at the SO?"

"I don't know where I am," I said. "I thought I was picking up a little consulting work from Mike Peralta while I tried to find a new teaching job. But universities aren't exactly clamoring to hire me. I got a letter from a dean at Arizona State last month, and he actually said I wrote too clearly to be taken seriously as an historian today."

"You're equal opportunity–challenged in these politically correct times, my love," she said.

"Tell me about it."

"It's no better in the news business; plus, we're run by these profit-driven corporate dickheads with their focus groups and readership surveys. We keep making stories shorter and dumber, and we wonder why nobody wants to read newspapers today. At least you know there will always be crime."

We ordered fish tacos, and I asked Lorie about Bobby Hamid.

"You tell me," she said. "Surely the Sheriff's Office intelligence files are piled high with Bobby Hamid information."

"You can give me a different perspective, as an award-winning reporter writing about organized crime."

"Yeah, shit," she snorted, then added, "He's a major, diversified scumbag. Tied in with new organized crime.

"Old organized crime—the Mafia—played by a code of sorts. For instance, they wouldn't murder cops or reporters. New organized crime—the Colombians, the Dominicans, the Samoans, the Russians, guys like Bobby Hamid—they'd just as soon kill you as look at you." Lorie spoke fast, talked with her hands. She was in her element now.

"Bobby has all sorts of alliances, keeps his hands in different products. Like he's tied in with the Aryan Brotherhood, distributing drugs in the Arizona State Prison. He uses the Mexican Mafia to terrorize competitors to his porno bookstores. I've heard he has his hands in reservation casinos, maybe through the old mob. He's an operator."

"Is he tied into flying drugs in from Mexico?"

"If he's not, somebody close to him is," Lorie said. "Bobby Hamid is like a Harvard Business School case study. He's a genius in maximizing the value of different enterprises—only these are illegal enterprises."

"So why has nobody ever shut him down?"

"Who knows? Another thing about the new organized crime is

how diffuse it is. The system is overwhelmed. I know your buddy Peralta has had a hard-on for Bobby for years, but . . . yeah, as I recall, the county attorney screwed the pooch a couple of years ago on a prosecution and Bobby walked. Had a very high-priced lawyer."

"Well," I said, "Bobby Hamid seems to keep turning up on the edges of my life."

She arched one eyebrow. "Is that why you ended up in a gunfight at Metrocenter last night?"

"You don't miss a thing, Ms. Pope."

"I didn't just fall off the turnip truck, Deputy Mapstone." It was one of our old routines from years ago.

I filled Lorie in from the beginning. I need someone to talk to, someone I trusted. When I was done, she shook her head slowly and said, "I should have known Julie Riding was involved in this somehow."

"Ironic, isn't it?"

"Ironic my ass," Lorie said, munching on a taco. "So let me get this straight: You go looking for your old girlfriend's missing sister, who ends up murdered in the desert, a dump arranged to look like the 1959 homicide you've been investigating. Little sister—Phaedra? That's a name—has a drug-mule boyfriend who also gets dead. Now you find out Phaedra was on the run for a month. And somebody with a large gun doesn't want you to find out why."

"That's about the size of it."

"I don't like it, David," Lorie said. "Something stinks."

I asked her what.

"Julie, for one thing," she said. "Your major source of information is addicted to blow, and now she's disappeared."

"I know she's all screwed up."

"In my business," Lorie Pope said, "we say, 'If your mother says she loves you, check it out.' "

"In my business, too," I said, and thought about what Harrison Wolfe had said about never confusing your prejudices with your instincts.

Lorie shook her head. "You're living quite the historical psychodrama, aren't you, Professor?" she asked. "Deputy in the old West—a paladin, if you will—fights for former lady love's honor."

"That's not it," I replied a bit too testily.

We finished our food in silence, surrounded by the din of the business-lunch crowd talking deals, sports, and gossip. At the next table, a trim middle-aged man was holding forth on the new roster for the Suns, how things had never been right since they traded Barkley. He said he'd played golf with Charles only yesterday. At another table, three women were talking about a shooting in one of their neighborhoods. Then Lorie picked up the tab and we walked back slowly, drifting past the tourist shops—flags, hot peppers, T-shirts, Indian art, *Arizona Highways*—staying in the shade.

"I was going to ask you how your love life is going," Lorie said finally, "but I guess I have my answer."

"I'm not sleeping with Julie," I said. Technically true. Haven't slept with her for a week. Why was I covering up? "I don't even know where she is." Too true.

"Mmm."

"I have a friend," I volunteered. "Kind of a work friend. We're not even dating, really. But it feels nice to be with her."

"Mmmhmm."

"And you?"

She paused by a shop window and studied us reflected in the glass. "Oh, I don't know." She walked on. "We never really know anybody. And our expectations for forever are so out of place. I mean, when humans needed the family unit to survive and only lived to be forty, monogamy made sense."

"You've drunk deep at the social science well," I said.

She smiled. "I've been in love so many times, or at least I thought I was in love. Next time, I'd like to find a friend, maybe, before I get all obsessive and self-destructive. Remember how that is?" She laughed.

I thought about that and said, "I guess I have love vertigo. Ever since my marriage ended. If I get too high up, I just get dizzy."

"Why did Patty leave you?" Lorie asked. "Sorry. Asking uncomfortable questions at the most inopportune time is an occupational hazard."

We were at the door to the *Republic*.

"It's okay," I said. "My occupational hazard is getting shot at. I don't know why. Maybe she fell in love with her boss. He owned a sailboat. Maybe the thought of being married to me for the rest of her life was too boring to contemplate. Now she's living with a twenty-two-year-old tennis pro. She never gave me an explanation. She was a millionaire's daughter, and I was just me."

"I guess that's the way it was for me with Richard," she said. Husband number two. "I never knew why. I eventually made myself realize I'll never know why. And I know I've probably done as bad or worse to my lovers. We live in an age of so much disconnection." She gave a rueful laugh. "Here I am, one of the killers and one of the dead."

"I don't want to grieve for Patty," I said earnestly. "I wouldn't want the falseness of that life again." Lorie looked at me. "But," I said, "she had a way of getting under my skin that I miss, that I still seek elsewhere."

"So you don't want nice girls?"

"I was always a nice guy."

"Yes, you were." Lorie gave me a hug and said, "I'll do some sniff work on this, David, and call you in a couple of days. But Phaedra is the key to your mystery. You've got to get into her last days. Her recent history, you know? Not what Julie says happened. But what really happened."

Then she pushed through the door and was gone.

After sundown, I drove back to Tempe, where Susan Knightly's studio was still locked and dark. Most of the afternoon, I'd sat at home in the cool dimness of Grandfather's office, listening to Charlie Parker and listlessly grading badly written essays, waiting in vain for the phone to ring. Now I was antsy and needed to walk, even in the heat. In the lobby of the building that housed the studio, two security guards were talking as I walked past. I caught only the end of their conversation: "That's what love means!" one said. I stepped out and walked down Mill Avenue. Just a tall dark-haired man, officially unemployed, too near middle age and carrying a large revolver.

The street is the main drag through the old part of Tempe, near the university, but it had been rebuilt since I went to school. Pricey new office buildings, tourist boutiques, a multiplex theater, and exotic restaurants sat along what had once been a quintessential college-town street. Sidewalk cafés were cooled by elaborate systems that shot jets of mist into the superheated desert air. Even in the heat, Mill Avenue was crowded with people, mostly young and female, achingly sexy, wearing as little as possible. The sexual flux was so real, you could feel it. Tall, long-legged, tan goddesses who said something about the value of American nutrition in the last part of the twentieth century. Sweet young objects of desire. They never studied history in college voluntarily. They paid me no mind. This would have been part of Phaedra's world, at least when she got off work every day at the photo studio.

I started at one end of the street and worked my way south, hitting the bars and restaurants, showing the photograph of the red-haired woman with the intense stare. The bartenders, managers, and maître d's were all amazingly friendly and wanted to be helpful. One woman behind the bar of a seafood place wanted to know if this would be on *America's Most Wanted.* They all seemed to be from somewhere else and were eager to tell you about how much they loved the Valley. There was just one problem: None remembered Phaedra. As one older woman said, "There are too many beautiful women in Phoenix. Who can keep track?"

Until I got to a coffee place across from the Gilbert Ortega Indian art store. There, a brooding young man with a goatee and three earrings in one ear nodded slowly when I showed him the photo.

"She'd come in for an iced grande mocha," he said deliberately.

"You're sure it's her?"

"I remember. I have a thing for redheads." He smiled vaguely and stared out at the street. "There's something mystical about redheads. And I thought she had a cool name. It'd be a great name for a band."

"You ever ask her out?"

He shook his head. "Didn't have the guts. She seemed too intense for me. A real bagful of emotions, you know? A little voice in me said, You don't want to go there."

I asked him if she always came in alone. He rubbed his stubbled chin. "Once she came in with another red-haired woman. She was older. Had a bunch of photo equipment on her shoulder. Seemed like they were friends."

He cleaned some metal canisters. "Then a couple of weeks ago, she met somebody here."

"Phaedra came in with somebody?"

"No," he said. "Phaedra came in alone and ordered. This woman came in after her and they talked at a table for a few minutes."

"What did she look like?"

"Not bad-looking, if she hadn't had such a hard look in her eyes. Older. Kinda light brown hair, straight, but pulled back." He thought about it for a moment. "She called her Julie. Phaedra did."

I felt a little sizzle at the back of my neck.

"You're sure this was two weeks ago?" I asked. "Not a month ago, maybe?"

"It would have been the Monday before last," he said. "I remembered how upset she seemed."

"You okay?" he asked.

"Yeah," I said. "Fine. What was Phaedra like? Glad to see the woman?"

"No, man. She seemed really agitated, now that I think about it. Spilled part of her coffee. They sat back there"—he pointed to a table—"for maybe five minutes. They were really into it. Phaedra was waving her hands, pushing back her hair—you know, the way pretty long-haired women do? Rubbing her eyes. Whatever this other chick was saying was upsetting her."

"What happened next?"

"They left."

"Together?"

He nodded.

"You have a good memory," I said.

"I'm in criminology at ASU," he said. "I want to get into the FBI. That's all I've ever wanted to do."

Lose the stubble and earrings, I thought. Or maybe not. The world keeps changing.

"You want to know who she was seeing? The redhead? My buddy Noah did ask her out, and I guess they hit it off. I didn't know if I should tell you, but you seem okay." I wrote down Noah's address and phone number.

"I hope she's not in trouble," he said as I turned to go.

I walked out into the hot evening and finally had the "Oh shit!" moment I had been working up to for several days, since Julie first disappeared. I realized that, divorced from my sentimental feelings about her, I didn't know Julie Riding very well at all. She'd told me she had joint custody of her daughter, but in reality, she had lost custody. She'd told me cocaine was in her past, but now I knew it was part of her present. She'd told me she hadn't seen her sister for a month before Phaedra turned up murdered, but a witness had just placed Julie with Phaedra the night before the body was found. I had argued with Peralta to protect Julie—because I know her—but it occurred to me with sudden, awful clarity that I didn't know her, not really. And I didn't know what I didn't know.

Oh shit.

Noah wasn't home, so I headed back to my house empty-handed. I was already out of sorts when the phone rang a little after 10:00 P.M.

"I didn't know if I should just leave you alone or not," said Lindsey.

"I'm sorry," I said. "I should have called." It was a cliché. And there was an edge in my voice.

"No," she said. "No reason for you to worry about that. But I heard about what happened last night. . . ."

"I'm okay. It was over pretty quickly."

"I know," she said, and the line was silent. Over the air-conditioning, I could actually hear a train whistle from down at the Santa Fe yards.

"Oh, Lindsey," I began. I thought, How I wish you were in my arms on this lonely, desolate night. Silence again.

"I think I may have found something you'll be interested in," she said finally, her voice different. "Something relating to Rebecca Stokes."

"That's great, Lindsey. What have you got?"

"Come by on Monday and I'll show you."

"Okay. Are you all right?"

"I'm fine, Dave. Get some rest."

I started to call her right back, but the phone rang.

"Lindsey?"

"You've replaced me already, my love?"

I sat up uneasily. "Where are you, Julie?"

"I'm around, David. I can't tell you right now. Soon we'll be together."

"Julie, we need to talk," I said.

"I suppose Peralta is threatening to arrest me."

"I don't really know," I said sharply. "I'd rather know why you met Phaedra down at a coffee place on Mill Avenue the night before she was found dead."

"David, I don't know what you're talking about. I haven't seen Phaedra for almost two months."

"Why this game, Julie? Who are you running from?"

"Maybe the same man as you, judging from the story in the *Republic* this morning." She was in the state at least, if she'd read the story today in the newspaper.

Julie said, "Haven't you thought about what I said to you, David? I'm really in love with you."

I said nothing. The line buzzed emptily.

"Don't you think we could try to make something happen here?" she said. "I mean, finally make something go right in our lives?"

"Does the name Bobby Hamid mean anything to you?"

"No, David. You don't understand. In time, I'll tell you what I know."

"Why can't you tell me now, Julie?"

"I just can't." The line went dead.

I slammed the phone down and cursed the walls.

"Rebecca Stokes was pregnant when she was murdered."

"What are you talking about?" I was standing in Lindsey's cubicle in the Central Records Division. I sat down. She was all in black: black T-shirt, black jeans, black boots. Even her lipstick was dark.

I'd spent a restless weekend, correcting papers and mulling over what I knew and didn't know. Then early Monday morning, I'd headed downtown to see Lindsey.

"There was an autopsy," she said, visibly pleased with herself. "The record was preserved."

"How? There was nothing like that in the case file. I assumed the autopsy report had been lost."

"You have to think outside the box, Dave." She adjusted her oval glasses, punched up several menus on her computer screen, and pointed.

"This was a research project in 1985 at the University of Arizona Medical School. A history of forensic pathology in Arizona in the 1950s, gleaned from autopsy records. And lo and behold, the autopsy of Rebecca Marie Stokes."

"You are amazing."

"It's all in the fingers." She opened a file, and we read silently together.

" 'A fetus, approximately eight weeks old, found in the womb,' " she read.

"Jesus Christ." I sat back.

"She was pregnant, Dave. That changes everything."

"Motive."

"Exactly. Killed by somebody she knew, like Harrison Wolfe said."

"So the lover was married and got his girlfriend, Rebecca, pregnant," I said.

"She refuses to have a back-alley abortion. He refuses to leave his wife," Lindsey said. "They argue. They fight. He kills her."

"If that's the real scenario," I said.

"You know it is, Dave," Lindsey put her hands on my knees, smiling widely. "She was a single middle-class woman living in 1959, and she was pregnant," Lindsey went on. "We know from Opal Harvey that she had a lover and he was a mystery man."

"So then," I said, "the question becomes, Who was he?"

I scrolled through the autopsy report, Lindsey leaning on my shoulder. It went into some detail about the crushing of the cricoid in her neck. The forensic serology report showed she'd had semen in her vagina.

"What about your friend Brent McConnico? Would he know who her lover was?" Lindsey asked.

"I doubt it," I said. "He was just a kid at the time. I guess it's worth asking, although I'm sure it won't make his day." I looked back at Lindsey. She was somewhere else.

"Do you think there's good and evil?" she said at last.

"I do," I said. "It's not very fashionable, I guess. The Holocaust and the gulag taught us there is radical evil."

"But is there good?"

"Of course," I said. "The soldiers who defeated the Nazis and liberated the death camps were good. A historian named Robert Conquest documented the millions of deaths in the Soviet Union, when most Western experts wanted to look the other way. I call that good." I stroked her wrist. "We're the good guys, aren't we?"

Lindsey looked at me with something like fondness. "I used to think, people don't even think these thoughts I do. . . . But you do."

I almost leaned over and kissed her. I said, "You are my hero, Lindsey. This really changes everything. Even if it blows my theory of a serial killer all to hell."

"There was a serial killer, Dave. He probably just wasn't involved in the Stokes murder."

"Right," I said. I felt awkward and silly. "You want to do something this week? Maybe see a movie?"

"I thought you'd never ask."

Back at home, I placed a call to Brent McConnico, left a message with his secretary, and settled into the big leather chair with a large Bloody Mary and my notes and files from the library. Phaedra was still in the center of my mind, but Lindsey's find on the Stokes case had fired me up. I was still going to earn my thousand dollars from Peralta, and even do some honest scholarship to boot.

Going through the notes I'd made on Governor McConnico, I was struck by how the murder of his niece could be seen as a turning point in his career. He was only about fifty when she disappeared, and he was seen as a rising star in the Democratic party. Newspapers of the time talked about him seeking the Senate in 1958. Instead, McConnico retired and went into corporate law with his longtime adviser, Sam Larkin. It seemed an odd turn, even if, as Brent McConnico had said, they never felt safe after Rebecca was killed. Indeed, newspapers and historical accounts didn't make the connection between Stokes and McConnico at all. Something else I didn't realize: Governor McConnico had died by his own hand in 1968.

I also looked through the Phoenix PD history, hoping for some insight into the department that had investigated Rebecca's murder. Names and dates and innovations—the first motorcycle unit, first helicopter patrol—but little on major cases. Just a sleepy desert town in the 1950s. And nothing on a detective from Los Angeles named Harrison Wolfe. I guess we'd used up our ration of luck for one day.

* * *

The phone rang at three o'clock, and I thought it might be Brent McConnico. Instead it was an impossibly young voice identifying himself as Noah Hunter. He sounded harried and apprehensive. When I asked about Phaedra, he was silent a long time. Then he said I could meet him on his work break that night at Planet Hollywood, where he was employed as a waiter.

It must have been 115 degrees outside, but the sun had disappeared behind the White Tank Mountains and a long line had gathered outside Planet Hollywood. The restaurant sat at one end of the Biltmore Fashion Park, an outdoor shopping mall in tony northeast Phoenix. I bypassed the line and heard some grumbling. The blond goddess at the front counter, backed by a life-size poster of Arnold, Bruce, and Demi, started to admonish me, but I discreetly showed my badge and asked for Noah Hunter. I was feeling too goddamned old to be waiting in lines in the heat when I didn't even want to be there.

In a moment, Noah Hunter appeared and steered me outside. We walked in silence toward a Coffee Plantation in the middle of the mall. He looked about twenty, tall and good-looking, with close-cropped light brown hair, a sensual mouth, and bad posture.

"They're gonna think I'm in trouble," he said sulkily.

"You can explain to them," I said.

We went inside and ordered iced mochas, then went back out to the sidewalk tables, which were cooled somewhat by the ever-present misters in the roof. He sprawled out across one of the chairs and casually regarded a young brunette walking past. She gave him a dazzling smile and tossed her head.

"So what do you want?"

"I want to talk about Phaedra Riding."

"It was that goddamned Josh, wasn't it?" He shook his head. "Cop wanna-be. Jesus."

"Do you know where Phaedra is?"

He looked me over and thought about copping an attitude. "No," he said.

"She's dead," I said, watching him carefully. "Murdered."

He sat up in a hurry. Then he rolled his head around violently. Tears welled up in his eyes. "What are you talking about, man? What are you talking about?"

I gave him the details and watched his eyes while he ignored his coffee and absently rubbed his neck with a large tanned hand.

"When was the last time you saw her?" I asked. I should have read him his rights, but I knew he didn't do it. I didn't tell him that.

"Shit, you think I killed her? Is that what you think?"

"If I thought that, I'd be here with lots of help," I said. "But your behavior is telling me I might have been wrong."

He stared at me.

"I'm listening."

He sighed and slumped into his chair. "Phaedra." He shook his head. "Such a cool, sexy name. She would come into this coffee place on Mill Avenue and just sit at the back and read. One day, I walk back there and she's reading John Stuart Mill. How do you start a conversation based on that?"

I could, I thought absently.

"But I got her talking and we hit it off, you know? So I asked her out, and we had a good time."

"When was that?"

"I don't remember exactly. School was still in session. Maybe late April."

"So you dated?"

He nodded.

"She was way too smart for me. Read about a book a day, seemed like. She also played the cello. Not your typical party chick. But she wasn't looking for anything heavy. I think she'd just come out of a relationship. We just had fun."

"When was the last time you saw her?"

He was silent and stared down at his hands.

"I can't believe she's dead." He shook his head. "She was such a sweet, gentle soul. Who would have killed her?"

"You tell me."

He stared at his hands. It was quiet enough that I could hear the hiss of the misters overhead. Off on Camelback Road, the traffic gave off a low roar.

"She came to me after school was over and asked if she could stay for a few weeks. I said sure."

"When was this?"

"June. Around the end of the month." He paused.

"She was scared, man," he said. "She was running from something."

"What?"

"I don't know." He looked at me. "You've got to believe me. I really don't know. When Phaedra didn't want to talk about something, she could send you to Siberia, you know? But she was real emphatic about me not telling anybody she was staying with me."

He took a draw on the iced mocha. "Phaedra was a very passionate, very unhappy person," he said. "Some people are just born disaffected. That was Phaedra. She was so damned deep, it was scary. And there was so much about her that was so wonderful—God, when she played her cello for me." He shook his head. "But there was so much she wouldn't talk about."

"Did you guys do drugs?"

"Shit no! You think I'm crazy? Yeah, I did a little ecstasy and pot when I was in high school. But not now. And you couldn't even talk to Phaedra about drugs. She'd go nuts."

So why was she involved with a drug pilot? I thought.

I asked, "How long did she stay?"

"Almost a month. It was really nice to have her there. She left two weeks ago. She made a phone call one day and said she needed to meet somebody. She didn't come back."

"You weren't worried?"

"I was worried," he said. "But she said it would be okay, when she went out that night. Anyway, I always figured she would just up and leave me one day. I got the sense that was the way she operated with men, you know? I didn't know anything was wrong."

"What about her car?"

He shook his head. "She didn't have a car. That was one of the things that was odd about her. She was always on foot. She said she had to lend her car to her sister."

I thanked him, a little too curtly, and left a business card. I said other deputies would be in touch.

He stared at me hard, like a young man challenged over his woman. And then his face changed, reddened, fell apart. I thought of the word *shattered* and where it must have come from, when the pain gets so great that it shatters. He cried like a little boy.

"The night before she left, she said she wanted to run away." He sobbed. "She asked me to go with her. I should have done it. . . ."

I let him cry. I put a hand on his shoulder and felt a deep emptiness in my middle.

The next morning, I was standing in the little rotunda of the Arizona capitol, under the restored copper dome, waiting for Brent McConnico. The capitol was modest and charming, the best effort of a frontier state that probably had fifty-thousand people and not much money when it entered the union in 1912. It compared favorably with the "new" building attached to it, a monument to 1970s architectural ugliness.

The night before, I'd typed up what I had learned so far about Phaedra. Soon I would have to take it in to Peralta. But I wasn't ready yet. Something made me want to talk to Susan Knightly before Peralta's detectives descended on the case.

Behind me was a hubbub of voices as people spilled out of a conference room. Brent McConnico was walking slowly down the corridor, deep in conversation with another man, his arm around the man's shoulders. He smiled toward me and raised a finger: Just a moment. Then he broke away and strode over, extending his hand.

"David," he said. "So good of you to work around my schedule. I have just about fifteen minutes; then I'm in appropriations hearing hell for the rest of the day."

He led me up a wide flight of stairs and into a deserted alcove overlooking the rotunda. "That was once the governor's office," he said pointing, "before they moved it into that monstrosity behind us."

"I remember coming up here with my Cub Scout troop," I said. "I think Paul Fannin was governor then."

"Ah yes, good old Paul," he said. "A great Arizonan."

I made some apologies and got to the point, explaining why his cousin's murder might not be a closed case. His face changed subtly, and he listened intently.

"Oh, come, come, David," he said. "Surely you don't believe this man, this retired detective? Sounds like he's doing some overdue ass-covering."

"I might think so, too, Senator, if it weren't for some new evidence we've run across."

"Call me Brent," he said quickly. "What evidence? What are you talking about?"

"We've interviewed a neighbor who knew Rebecca, and she said Rebecca had a secret lover."

"A secret lover?" He laughed a little too loudly. "Where on earth did that come from? I've never heard of such a thing."

I just looked at him earnestly.

"And even if it were true," he said, "what does that have to do with anything?"

"The lover might have killed her. We know now her murder didn't fit the Creeper pattern."

"Oh, David, that's quite a stretch, I think. You're a little obsessed with this, don't you think?"

"Brent, your cousin was about two months pregnant when she was murdered."

The blood ran out of his fine bronze tan. He opened his mouth, but no words came out. I shouldn't have tried to tell him this in between meetings. He walked a couple of feet to a marble bench and sat, staring out into the rotunda. A babble of voices traveled upward.

"I'm sorry," I said. "I know it must be a shock."

He stood and walked away. "I can't discuss this anymore today," he said.

"I just need to know—"

He turned violently, his face red. "You need?" his voice was strident; then he lowered it. "You need?" he hissed. "You've caused my family quite enough pain with this . . . this ego-aggrandizing fishing expedition, Deputy!"

He turned and strode angrily off. I guess we weren't on first-name basis any longer.

I walked the two blocks through the lushly landscaped capitol grounds to the visitors' parking lot, wondering how I might have handled that better. The case wasn't merely a historical inquiry; it was a real murder, with real family members left behind, people who'd been hurt. I climbed into the Blazer, took the sunshade out of the windshield and the towel off the steering wheel, and started the engine. That was when I saw a man in a charcoal gray suit walk quickly out of one of the side entrances and head toward a parking area. It was Brent McConnico.

He climbed into a silver BMW convertible and sped out of the lot, a cellular phone stuck to his face. I was already moving, and I fell in behind him about half a block back. I can't say why, but something in his movements wasn't right. And a BMW was a strange place to be holding an appropriations committee meeting.

He drove up Seventh Avenue to the on-ramp of the Papago Freeway, blowing past the homeless person selling papers at the light, heading east. I had to speed up to avoid losing him. He was moving, doing at least eighty. I closed the gap, so I was maybe six car lengths behind him in moderately heavy traffic. His Arizona personalized plate said YALE N 3.

At the Squaw Peak Parkway, he turned north. I followed behind, maintaining a steady ninety-five as we left behind the mere mortals in the slow lanes. I hoped the Blazer's engine, emasculated for California smog regulations, would hold together. The sun glinted off the BMW as we entered nicer and nicer neighborhoods, then rolled past expansive houses sitting on the sides of cliffs and mountains.

He turned east again on Shea Boulevard and pulled into a little strip mall. I drove on past about a block and doubled back, parking at a Carl's Jr. restaurant across the street. He didn't have a clue what I drove, anyway. He was sitting in the parking lot with the engine going. He sat like that for maybe ten minutes. Then a black Mustang with dark-tinted windows pulled in beside him and a man I'd seen before got out and climbed into the passenger side of the BMW.

The last time I'd seen that short, muscular man, he was pointing a machine gun at me.

My heart was pounding. I could unholster the Python and walk across the street, Dirty Harry–style. Or I could call for backup.

I did neither. This was all just too damned strange. I picked up the cell phone and called Lindsey.

"Hi, beautiful."

"Dave, you made me day."

"Guess what I'm doing?"

"Uh, writing about the effect of the Great Depression on the Rocky Mountain states?"

"Close," I said. "I'm watching the majority leader of the state senate talking to the man who tried to blow me away at Metrocenter the other night." I read her the license plate of the Mustang and heard her emphatically typing it in.

"Hang on," she said. "The system's been down all day. Are you safe? They can't see you?"

"I'm across the street."

"You want backup? I can roll PD."

"Not yet," I said.

"Okay, we have liftoff," she said, then read me the information. I wrote it down and then watched them inside the BMW. Brent McConnico was gesturing violently as the small, muscular man sat impassively.

"Thanks. You're my hero again."

"I'm speaking in clichés," Lindsey said. "But be careful."

"I will. We've got plans tomorrow night." I hung up.

Across the street, the muscular man, whose name was apparently Dennis Copeland, got out of the BMW and closed the door. Then McConnico waved him back to the driver's side, rolled down the window, and spoke again. Dennis Copeland dismissed him with a wave, climbed into the Mustang, and roared off. I pulled in behind him and got on the cell phone.

We descended back into the Valley on the Squaw Peak Parkway and exited at Indian School Road, going the speed limit. I held steady about half a block behind the Mustang. We were headed toward Central when my cell phone squealed.

"Deputy Mapstone, look behind you." A Phoenix cop was on my tail. "I'm Officer Brenda Jackson. Chief Peralta tells us you need some help."

"It's the black Mustang just ahead of me," I said, pushing it to make the light at Sixteenth Street. She was still with me. "He's the guy from the Metrocenter shooting."

"How long has it been since you've done a felony traffic stop?" Brenda Jackson wanted to know.

"A little while," I said, lying. It had been fifteen years. "But it's like riding a bicycle."

She laughed. "We'll pick up another unit at Central and then we'll box him. I want you to be on his outside as we rope him in. By that time, other units should be with us. If he starts to run, let him go at a distance."

"Ten-four," I said.

He continued westbound on Indian School Road and crossed Central almost leisurely. Just as Brenda Jackson had said, I saw another PPD cruiser in the rearview mirror. He came up very quickly and passed us all, positioning himself ahead of the Mustang. Traffic was fairly thin. The sidewalks were deserted and few buildings were close to the street. It wouldn't get any better than this.

"Let's do it," Jackson said.

I pulled into the outside lane and punched the accelerator to close the gap with the Mustang. Jackson came right up on his tail and hit the emergency lights. Then the cruiser ahead slowed suddenly. I pulled up beside the Mustang and the trap was closed. All I could see through the dark tint of the windows was the outline of a man.

Jackson hit her siren and he was forced to slow again by the cruiser right ahead of him. Then he slammed on the brakes, and we were all out of our cars, facing him with pistols drawn and automobiles between us and him.

"Driver of the Mustang," Jackson announced on the PA system. "Roll down your windows so we can see you. If you have any weapons, throw them out on the driver's side. Keep your hands where we can see them. Slide across and get out on the passenger side—repeat, the passenger side. Keep your hands in plain sight."

A long time seemed to pass as cars whizzed by behind me. She repeated the order. The driver just sat there behind his dark windows. A thought crept into my head: What if it's the wrong guy? The cop from the lead car edged in toward the Mustang, semiautomatic pistol drawn. He was tall, skinny, blond, and very young.

Then his face just disappeared in a mist of blood and smoke and the splinters of his sunglasses, followed by a massive boom and echo. His body snapped backward and fell heavily to the pavement.

I squeezed off a round, the big Python jumped in my hand, and the window on the driver's side of the Mustang exploded from the impact of the .357. But Copeland was already moving fast, kicking open the passenger door and rolling out onto the sidewalk. I couldn't see him.

"He's going east on foot!" Jackson yelled. I could see her talking into her walkie-talkie, calling for assistance. I scuttled low around the Blazer and the police cruiser in front of the Mustang. The young cop was flat on his back and his face was gone. I felt for a carotid pulse in the gore. Nothing. I was shaking, and I thought very clearly, Copeland must have shot through the windshield of the Mustang.

Then the side windows of the police cruiser came apart and bullets were whizzing past me. I fell to the asphalt and immediately got burned from the heat. I rolled and rose to a crouch. I could see his feet. Then I didn't know where he was. Somewhere on the other side of the police car, maybe. Or maybe coming toward me.

I heard Brenda Jackson on the other side of the cars, ordering him to freeze. I rose, still separated by two vehicles, and watched him turn toward her, a long-barreled .44 Magnum in one hand and my old friend the machine gun in the other, both traveling upward. Three quick cracks. She was firing.

"Fuck, he's got body armor!"

He fired a burst from the machine gun, and she went down, groaning, squeezing off more rounds herself. I fired in his direction but couldn't get a good aim because of the sun. I felt terrified and useless. I fired again, and he fell to the ground.

Then part of the cruiser's light bar disintegrated as he fired the Magnum at me. A *ka-boom* and the echo, more like artillery than a pistol. The lead cruiser's back window blew out and the bullet kept going, smashing into a sign across the street. I scuttled and crawled counterclockwise toward the back of the cars.

I backed up to Jackson, the Python at the ready. I still didn't know if he'd run or try to finish us off. She was back against the rear bumper, sliding a new magazine in her semiautomatic pistol.

"I'm okay," she mouthed. But she was bleeding. "Go!" she whispered, nodding toward Copeland.

I fought off my fear and came out low and fast on the other side of the cruiser. But he was gone. I ran east on Indian School Road. One block, two. I ran and crouched, ran again and crouched. The heat burning in my lungs, I scanned the low-rise office buildings and condos for a sign of him. Nothing. I could hear sirens coming up the street behind me.

* * *

My first memory of a police officer being killed in the line of duty was when I was ten years old. A motorcycle cop was shot at a traffic stop near downtown Phoenix, and another motorcycle officer responding to the call for assistance was killed when a car ran through an intersection and hit him. It happened at Seventh Avenue and Roosevelt, not all that far from our home, in a city that seemed miles removed from the riots and mayhem of the 1960s. The photos of the two dead cops were on the evening news for days afterward, and it seemed unalterably grave and sad. I remember Grandfather, who had many old-fashioned notions, saying that killing a police officer in the line of duty was the worst crime because it was an attack on society itself.

Ten years later, when I joined the strange, closed world of the police, it was not so rare for cops to be murdered. We started wearing flak vests and carrying backup firearms. I remember one winter night when a two-man unit stopped a car at a citrus grove south of Guadalupe, not knowing it held two prison escapees from Oklahoma. The convicts had automatic weapons and the .38-caliber revolvers of the deputies were no match. Both deputies were two years away from retirement. We pulled up with the gun smoke still in the air, and Peralta jumped out of the car with a pump-action shotgun before I could even open my door. It was the first time I really saw his fury. He killed both cons where they stood, a surreal scene, like something out of a Western. And he said just what Grandfather had: To kill a cop in the line of duty was to attack society itself.

My mind returned to the young officer obliterated by the man in the Mustang. In the line of duty. Duty was an increasingly quaint idea to most Americans. My colleagues in academia scoffed at such a notion. But it must have at least partly inspired this young man to take a job paying $27,000 a year, where the most he could hope for was to be spat upon and called a pig as his marriage crumbled and his debts grew. His name was Glenn Adams, he was twenty-four, and he had a new wife. All his hopes and dreams ended on Indian School Road on an ordinary summer afternoon.

In a few days, I would put on my uniform for the first time in a decade and a half. I would drape my gold star with a bar of black tape and join my comrades at Glenn Adams's funeral. We would honor his sacrifice and vow to keep him in our memory always. It is what we would hope for ourselves.

A half hour before midnight, I finally headed home from Madison Street. Was it still Tuesday night? I couldn't even remember. The term *bone-tired,* I understood.

I'd been through several hours of interviews with the Internal Affairs team from Phoenix PD, then the IAD investigators from the Sheriff's Office (who were wondering who the hell I was). Then the Public Affairs officers from both departments: The TV stations were all leading their newscasts with "Cop killing on city street in broad daylight." Then came several layers of brass, asking the same questions over and over. The Sheriff himself came to ask some questions, patted me on the shoulder, and then left to brief the reporters waiting in his pressroom.

Then an extended private ass-kicking from Peralta: Why had I been following Brent McConnico? How could I be sure Dennis Copeland was the same man I'd seen at Metrocenter? Why hadn't I waited until more backup was available? How could I have let such inexperienced officers try to stop Copeland? Why was I such a bad shot? How could I have let Copeland escape—twice? And—the heart of the matter—why did I "screw the pooch," as he called it, with his bête noire, the Phoenix Police Department?

It was a bad scene, as we used to say in the sixties. Peralta had moved past his demonstrative anger—the shouting and thundering and pounding on his desk—into a barely controlled rage of pedantic lectures and nasty questions, over and over. It was Mike Peralta at his worst. The Brent McConnico factor left an especially bad taste in my mouth. Peralta claimed to disbelieve that McConnico had even been at the strip mall on Shea Boulevard, meeting Dennis Copeland. I wasn't my best, either. I accused Peralta of soft-pedaling McConnico's role to preserve his own political skin. That started him all over again. The only thing that saved me was Peralta being summoned to a disturbance at the jail. I'd had enough for one day.

I walked down the dimly lighted corridor totally spent. I was exhausted and sore. The palms of my hands hurt from the 130-degree temperature of the asphalt I'd hit earlier that day. Even my ankles hurt.

In a little alcove by the elevator, Lindsey was sitting with her feet propped up on another chair, dozing. In sleep, there was something darkly reassuring about her beauty, gold stud in her nose and all. I sat down beside her and gently brushed her hair away from her face. The indirect light caught the rich browns and auburns in what had first appeared to be nearly black, fine, straight hair. My raven. She smiled and sighed and stretched.

"Hey, Dave," she said. "I figured you could use a friend."

"You figured right," I said.

"I told you to be careful."

"I tried."

She reached out her hand and I pulled her up. We took the elevator and escaped into the night.

We went to her apartment in Sunnyslope, where we sat on an old couch covered with a comforter, drinking Chardonnay, listening to angry young music, and talking for hours.

She had a cat, a big languid gray tabby named Pasternak, reflecting a late-teen obsession with Russian literature and history. We talked about *Dr. Zhivago* and Lindsey said she had always been touched by the character of Lara, wrenched from love and doomed by revolution. In the movie, there was the streetcar scene, of course, where Yuri and Lara see each other years later but are hopelessly separated by time and motion.

I always remembered Zhivago's brother, the Soviet officer, who talked about how Yuri and Lara were among the millions murdered to realize the Communist ideal, which of course was a sham. Tens upon tens of millions killed in this bloodiest of centuries, all in the service of murderous ideologies that sought to kill even history—especially history!—a trail of inhumanity and rage and social disintegration, a steady return to barbarism that led even to Maricopa County, Arizona, and young women left dead in the desert.

This was the point at which my dating life usually self-destructed, but Lindsey stayed with me, for some odd reason genuinely interested. "I wish I could have studied history with you," she said.

The cat purred at my feet. I let it sniff my finger and then chucked it under the chin. "Pasternak likes you," she said. She took my hand and stroked it lightly, skin on skin, touch on touch. She had long, elegant fingers. "I do, too."

She held my hand against her warm lips and kissed it.

"I don't have any answers," I said.

"I don't want any." She ran a finger down my face, tracing the curve of my cheek, mapping out my lips.

I looked at her. Her eyes were a subtle blue, something I had not noticed before, overpowered by the monochromes of her dark hair and clothes and white skin.

"I don't know the human heart."

"I don't, either," she said, and kissed me lightly.

"I failed in my marriage," I said.

"Stop living in the past, History Shamus."

"I'm thirteen years older than you. I don't have movie-star looks or a sailboat. I don't even have a real job." I sighed. "I'm feeling pretty broken right now."

"I like the way you're broken," she said, and kissed me again, our tongues touching lightly. "I know what you are."

I started to open my mouth, but she put two fingers against my lips. "Shhhh."

And so I took her in my arms, Lindsey Faith Adams, and kissed her like I'd wanted to from the first second I ever laid eyes on her.

In the morning, I cooked us breakfast, Mexican omelettes and English muffins, and we sat in bed eating and reading about the shooting in the *Republic*. As usual, the media got the story only half-right. Pasternak went out on the balcony and provoked a mocking bird, who fussed at him loudly.

"So what's your unified field theory?" Lindsey asked.

"I prefer lying in bed with a beautiful naked woman, reveling in what a sexy, wonderful find she is," I said. I felt sore in all the right places, all the forgotten, out-of-practice places. "Out there!"—I nodded out the window—"they can all go to hell."

Lindsey ate a forkful of omelette. "This is very good, Dave."

"My theory?" I said. "Add Brent McConnico, the next governor, to our list of people who have landed in bad shit. I kept thinking this Copeland guy from the Metrocenter had to be tied into Phaedra's murder. But I guess—and here's where my theory runs out of track—he's connected to McConnico, which means he's connected to Rebecca Stokes, who was murdered forty years ago. But he's no damned ghost. . . ."

"Something from that long ago still matters," Lindsey said. She put some preserves on a piece of muffin and fed it to me. "Something matters enough to kill for."

"So we get a break in one case, and it knocks the legs out of the other one. Shit. I just need to let that go. Let Peralta throw Julie in jail forever."

She read my face and said, "You know this isn't going to be a happy ending with Julie, don't you, Dave? Are you sure you want to go there?"

I tried to smile. "You're pretty smart for a computer nerd."

"It's the database of the heart," Lindsey said.

"I'm with you," I said, kissing her hand. "It's where I want to be."

"I know," she said. "I'm glad for both of us."

Afterward, I took our plates to the kitchen and then climbed back into bed. Lindsey draped a long leg across me. Young, taut skin—the most amazing feeling.

"So let's tie up some loose ends," I said. "Why did Julie say she was being followed?"

"We know she's truth-challenged," Lindsey said. "But if she's on the level, maybe she first saw this guy Copeland when he was actually watching you." She smirked. "She obviously thinks every man wants her. Then Copeland sees Julie with you and decides to find out if she's important, so he follows her."

Lindsey was under the covers, kissing my calves, running her fingers up my thighs. The exquisite softness of her hair brushed against me. Every pore of my skin was tingling. All my reasoning powers ran away and I just wanted to feel her wonderful lips and mouth.

"What about—Oh God, that feels *so good*—what about Metrocenter? That was about Rebecca Stokes?"

Lindsey popped her head out of the covers. "It made sense to think Copeland was after Susan Knightly and Phaedra. Actually, it looks like he was after you."

"Then he really is a bad shot."

"And I'm glad of that, too." She smiled. "Now, stop thinking, Professor."

I lay back and did just that.

In a small street-side building in the shadow of Camelback Mountain is Vincent Guerithault, one of the best restaurants in a city that has finally developed a reputation for world-class dining. They say Vincent's is classy, not snobby. I guess so. On Sunday night, a twentysomething, goateed maître d' floated ahead of me through the restaurant's small rooms, leading me to a nearly empty nook in the rear. Brent McConnico rose gracefully and extended his hand.

"David, it was so good of you to come," he said. "Please, sit."

A waiter hovered silently, unfurling my napkin for me.

"I believe Dr. Mapstone will have a martini, Bombay Sapphire, as I recall. Very dry, right? One olive."

I nodded and the waiter went away. McConnico was drinking what looked like bourbon on the rocks.

"David, you must forgive me," he said. "I very much lost my head last Tuesday. I said some things I didn't mean. I want to make amends."

I made an apology, too. I hadn't meant to upset him about his cousin's murder. But that might be the least of his problems after tonight. Over the past four days, I'd learned a lot about Brent McConnico—things that started as rumors and legends, recalled by Lorie Pope over drinks at Durant's, then hardened into evidence with the help of Lindsey and hours spent gleaning obscure documents. For the moment, though, cordiality reigned.

"All can be forgiven," he said. I thought it was an interesting choice of words. "We all lose our heads. But you and I, we have a lot in common. We're both real Arizonans, for one thing."

"There aren't too many of us, I guess."

"No, there aren't," McConnico said. "I was reading a story in the *Republic* today about the professional sports teams. Do you realize Phoenix is one of eleven cities around the country that has all four major professional sports represented? God, I remember when the Suns first came to town, and that was all we had for years."

"I do, too. We went to a lot of games that first season. At the old coliseum. . . ."

Brent McConnico smiled past me. "Anyway, this article quoted some academic type—no offense—sneering about Phoenix's inferiority complex, and about how we're a city of Jed Clampetts building 'ce-ment ponds.' No culture. No philanthropy. No history. People like that don't understand this city, this state."

The waiter reappeared with the martini. Brent McConnico looked at him, annoyed, and he retreated.

"You and me, David, our families. They mortgaged their land to build the first dam so we'd have water in this Valley. People today, they don't even know where our water comes from, they take it so for granted. In our parents' lifetimes, this city was built. It's a miracle."

He was fairly drunk. He hid it well, until he got on a roll like this.

"David, I hope you don't mind, but I made some inquiries about you."

"I guess not."

"I felt so bad about what happened. I wondered what I might do to make things better between us."

"Senator, you don't owe me anything."

"Brent, please call me Brent."

"Brent."

"Anyway, David, you've got quite an interesting history, no pun intended. Raised by your grandparents after your parents were killed. A sheriff's deputy for four years in the early 1980s. Then you got your master's and Ph.D. in history and left Phoenix to teach. You went to Miami of Ohio for eight years, right? Then to San Diego State. What a beautiful city San Diego is."

The waiter took our orders. I ordered the lobster quesadilla. McConnico asked for another drink and the duck tamale with Anaheim chile and raisins.

"You wrote a modestly successful book on a history of American railroads. You were a popular teacher," he went on. "You didn't get on as well with some of your faculty colleagues, I understand. The politically correct types. God, I hate that kind of institutionalized intolerance." He started on the new drink. "Married for five years to an heiress to a beer fortune. Patricia? Divorced, no children. And now you're back in Phoenix, having turned forty. When most people are well settled down and connected, you're very alone."

I picked apart a roll and ate a piece. "I guess you did your homework, Brent," I said.

"I did that to help, David," he said. "You see, I have an interest in our university system, in the quality of education. It's been one of the centerpieces of my career. I would love nothing better than to see a native Arizonan come back home and do what he does best. You know, that's always been a problem in this state. We look outside for everything. We don't look after our own. We don't appreciate our homegrown talent."

He watched as a slender redhead walked past in a short black cocktail dress. She looked us over and smiled. I thought of Phaedra.

"Anyway, David, I've been talking to my good friend Charles Harrington, who, as you know, is the dean of the college of liberal arts at ASU. He tells me they'd love to talk to you about a tenured position in the History Department."

"That's interesting, Brent, considering that a month ago my alma mater wouldn't give me the time of day."

He waved it away with a wave of his elegant Yale-in-3 hand. "David, it's all who you know. This is a relationship-based world. You have to get the door opened, so people can see how smart and talented you are. It's in the bag, David. The job is yours. Just take it." He smiled warmly.

I sipped the martini, a truly sublime creation. I thought about what McConnico was saying. It brought to mind the line in Dante's *Inferno*: "For the straight path was lost." Or as an old cop used to say to me, "Who knows what happens to people?"

"Brent," I said. "Tell me about the Rico Verde Cattle Company."

His mouth tightened imperceptibly.

"Come again?"

"The Rico Verde Cattle Company."

"You're babbling now, David. Didn't you just hear what I'm offering you?"

"Rico Verde was a land swindle back in the mid-1980s, substantial even by Arizona standards. The profits were never found. A couple of people went to prison. But a newspaper reporter I know says the real kingpin of Rico Verde was a man named Sam Larkin."

Brent McConnico stared at me. His hand trembled and upset the bourbon. A puddle of liquor rolled across the tablecloth. The waiter silently cleared away the spill and brought another drink along with our food.

"Sam Larkin was your political mentor, if my history's correct. And the year Rico Verde went down, you were in need of money, so the scuttlebutt down at the newspaper goes. Something about a rape allegation involving a legislative page? It must have cost dearly to make her go away."

"You'd better stop right there, Mapstone," he said. His finely sculpted cheekbones were flushed.

"See, I couldn't understand the link between Rebecca's murder and you. I mean, you were just a kid when she was killed. But there had to be something. Something big enough to make you hire a goon named Dennis Copeland to warn me off, and, when I didn't take the hint, to kill me."

I leaned in toward him. "And I didn't understand why the things I said to you Tuesday upset you so badly that you got careless and drove straight from the capitol to meet the man in the black Mustang."

He stared at me, suddenly ashen. "You followed me?" he said.

"You drive fast."

"You little bastard," he said.

He was actually indignant, as if I'd shown up at his country club or tried to date his perfect WASP daughter.

"That man Copeland murdered a police officer after he left you. That makes you an accessory."

He shook his head deliberately. "I had nothing to do with that." He lowered his voice and spoke more calmly. "No one will believe you anyway. One phone call to Mike Peralta will end your little law-enforcement adventure, Mapstone. I tell nobodies like Mike Peralta what to do. I can step on you just like a bug."

"I don't doubt it," I said. "Which made Copeland even more puzzling to me. Why would somebody like you need muscle when you have all this power?"

"Well, what on earth do you theorize, Professor?" he asked with extravagant sarcasm. "Pray tell me what you see."

I looked at him hard and said, "I see a loser in debt to the mob."

I expected him to shout or break down, but he just leaned back and regarded me with a disdainful patrician calm. "You are a fool, David. Two minutes ago, you could have had a cushy job—teach a couple of classes, fuck the beautiful young coeds, draw a check from the taxpayers. Now . . ."

He paused and sipped his drink. Then he cut his food and began to eat.

"Now," he said pleasantly, "I am going fuck you like you have never been fucked. You won't be able to find work as a school janitor when I get through. And then one night, when your guard is down, dear socially challenged Dennis will be back, and you will die. He has a real sadistic streak."

I said, "The Rico Verde Cattle Company, Brent. . . ."

He shook his head and laughed softly. "You are very persistent, David."

"I have a thirst for knowledge."

"Yes, I suppose you do," he said. "Rico Verde was very good to me. My name wasn't associated with it, of course. But I made a tidy profit, which is essential for a young man with political ambition and no money." He was picking apart the dried-flower arrangement.

"What about your family's money?"

He snorted. "There was none. A college trust fund, tightly controlled. Then nothing. That was my old man. In the 1960s, everybody in America made money, except him. A former governor no less. He refused to profit from his name or connections. He was weak. Sam wasn't weak. Sam knew money and power. If that put him into debt with unsavory people, it was worth it."

"And if thousands of people bought Rico Verde land that didn't exist?"

"I guess I don't feel anything for them," McConnico said. "I hope they voted for me. I remember calling that year for very strict sanctions against the real estate frauds that were ruining our state."

"So you are a hypocrite as well as a crook."

"Oh, David, to ascribe hypocrisy is to assume there is a just God and a moral universe. We know that doesn't exist. If it did, where is my punishment? Where is your justice? History is written by the victors—isn't that what they say?"

"And what about your cousin, Rebecca?" I asked, feeling a numbness in my feet. "If you're a victor, how do you live with that, McConnico? Just a kid, really, came out west thinking she could get a little freedom but still be safe with her family. Easy prey for your 'strong man' Sam, right?"

He blinked at me twice, then blinked twice again. "Nobody knows what happened to Rebecca. You said it was a serial killer. I believe that."

"I believed it once," I said. "Then I found out about Rebecca's secret lover, a distinguished man who visited only at night. And I found out she was pregnant when she was killed. And I found out Sam Larkin came by his mob connections by marriage, so leaving his wife wouldn't have been healthy—even if he intended to do it."

"Sam helped her," he said, a hint of pleading in his voice. "When Dad got her the job at the law firm, she couldn't even type."

"Helped himself," I said harshly. "And when she came back from Chicago, knowing she was pregnant, she decided to confront him."

"He couldn't leave Aunt Louise!" he hissed. "Rebecca knew that!"

"First they made love. She'd been gone a month, after all. Then she told him she was pregnant. They fought. He flew into a rage."

"He never meant for it to happen!" McConnico hissed, boring into me with his eyes. "I'm the only one he ever told—when I was thirty years old. How do you think it made me feel! It was like this 'thing' I carried around inside me all these years. I wanted it all to go away—Jesus, I was a kid when this happened—and I thought it had. Then you show up."

There was a movement behind him, and Peralta slid out a chair and sat. McConnico looked disoriented. He looked at me and then at Peralta. For a long moment, all we heard was the luminescent hush that attaches to conversations in very expensive restaurants. McConnico's face grew so red, I thought he was going to have a stroke.

"You were recording this, weren't you?"

Peralta said, "Senator, you have the right to remain silent. . . ."

"Don't you Mirandize me, you son of a bitch!" he shouted. A waiter discreetly cocked his head in our direction.

"Anything you say can and will be used against you in a court of law. . . ."

"Peralta, your career is dead if you go through with this. Do you hear me!"

"You have the right to an attorney. . . ."

"If you want a future in politics in this state, Peralta, you are to forget this ever happened!"

"If you cannot afford an attorney, one will be appointed for you."

"I own your ass!" McConnico cried. "You do what I tell you! You are to leave this room and get the tape and bring it to me. If you don't . . ."

He stared at Peralta, who was impassive and grim. McConnico was breathing faster. "Senator," Peralta said, "let's step outside quietly."

More time passed. McConnico started to sob silently. "This isn't what you think, Mike."

"It's time to go."

"He's twisted everything," McConnico wagged a finger in my direction. "I had nothing to do with any of this!" He was outright bawling now, snot and tears running down his face. Peralta's expression hardened.

"Senator," he said. "Since you own my ass, you know that if you don't get out of that chair and walk outside quietly with me and Deputy Mapstone"—Peralta looked at me and his eyes smiled—"I'm going to handcuff you and carry you out like the sorry sack of shit you really are."

Peralta nodded to the waiter, who approached timidly. "Check, please."

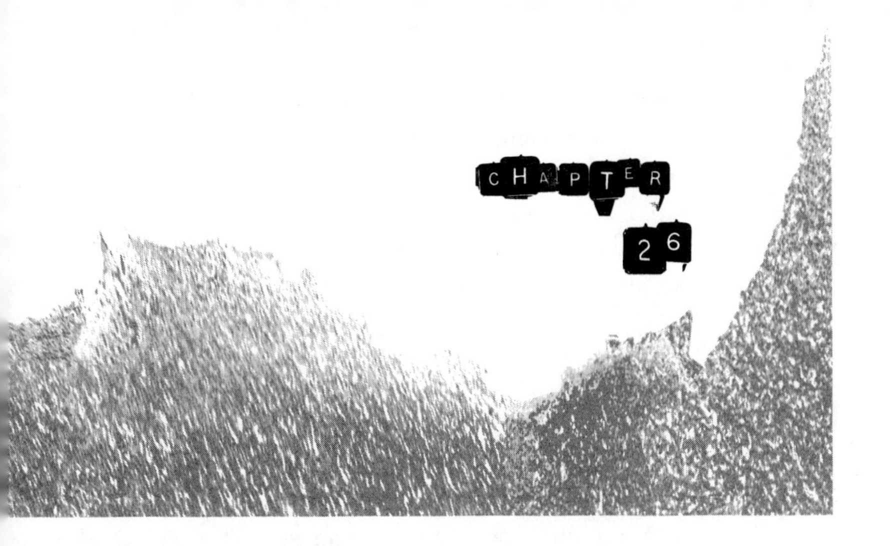

The next night, a big storm swirled in from the south and east. Thunderheads congregated over the Superstition Mountains and spilled north to the peaks of the McDowells. But they just hung in the sky, looking fat with rain and promise. I pulled off the Red Mountain Expressway and turned north into Scottsdale, cursing the unchanging heat in the city. Maybe we would end up like the Hohokam. Maybe all our cleverness couldn't overcome the eternal logic of the desert. The wind pushed a tumbleweed across the expensive crosswalk brickwork of Scottsdale Road. I veered onto Goldwater Boulevard and found the address Lorie Pope had given me.

It was an old adobe house, set back from the exclusive galleries that lined the street. A relic of the old farm village of Scottsdale, soon to be gobbled up by the wealthy appetite of the world-famous resort city. I drove slowly past, pulled around the corner, and got out. I had the Colt Python and two speed loaders on my belt. I didn't have to do this alone. Shouldn't have, by Peralta's later reckoning. But somehow, the past month had created its own little obsessive clockwork inside me. I was ready to see things through now—wherever they led.

The door to the adobe was ajar. I was about to push my way through, when I heard men's voices.

"I can't believe you're still alive. You're like some devil that won't die." It was an old-man's tenor voice, driven as much by breath as by vibration of vocal chords. I sank back into the shadows of the porch.

"None of this had to happen," the voice said. "If that Mexican sheriff and that goddamned history teacher hadn't gotten back into it. In my day . . ." He chuckled, an odd, unsettling rumble. "Well, in my day, you knew what would happen."

Silence. A very long silence. The wind whipped against the door and made it creak. The adobe felt rough and reassuring against my hand.

"I've got nothing to confess to you," the voice went on. "You don't scare me. You didn't scare me forty years ago. That girl's death was an accident. You know that. I didn't mean to grab hold of her the way I did. It's just that she went crazy, just like a wild animal."

The other man said something I couldn't make out.

Then the old man's tenor rasped, "My God, I had a wife and a family. I had a law practice and standing in the community. Things were different then. She wanted too much. We could have settled things. But she wanted too much. I am so goddamned sorry it was John Henry's niece, so goddamned sorry. I tried to make it up to him, to his son. But that's all in the past. Killing me won't change one minute of it."

I unholstered the Python and stepped into the room. It was a small front room, made smaller still by stacks of law books and newspapers, by the halfhearted light of a tattered floor lamp. One man sat deflated in an old chair. Everything about him was the color of cigarette ash: his loose skin, the wisps of hair ringing his bald head, even the old-man pants and shirt that were now too big for him. The other man was Harrison Wolfe.

Wolfe said, "Mapstone, meet Sam Larkin." He added distastefully, "The Kingmaker."

"You don't need that," Wolfe said, indicating the Python. "My God, that's a piece of artillery." Stuck in his belt, Wolfe had a Smith & Wesson .38-caliber Chief's Special: old-fashioned, compactly lethal. I holstered the big Colt.

Wolfe said, "You're thinking, I didn't even know Sam Larkin was still alive. Well, I thought the same thing until you stirred this up again. Then after you and I met, somebody's muscle started following me. That got me to thinking, Who would give a tinker's damn about this case after all this time? And I knew I had to pay a visit to old Sam here. He looks every one of his eighty-seven years, doesn't he?"

Larkin regarded me with watery eyes. "You could have left well enough alone."

"I needed a job," I said. "Now I think that Mexican sheriff is going to want to talk to you."

"Nobody's talking." It was a new voice, coming from behind me. The next thing I felt was a gun barrel push me into the room. I turned, to see Dennis Copeland. His eyes were like burned glass.

Larkin laughed until he started wheezing and coughing.

"My associate arrived just in time," he gasped.

"He doesn't work for McConnico?" I demanded, mustering a bravado I didn't feel, looking down the barrel of a .44 Magnum. The Python was now a hand's grasp away—might as well have been a light-year.

"You're a young fool," Larkin spat at me. "This man works for me. If you'd have paid attention to him, none of this would have happened."

He ran a bony hand across his bald crown. "Brent is a young fool, too."

I noticed Harrison Wolfe again when he subtly shifted his weight and faced Copeland.

Wolfe said, "Mr. Copeland, you murdered a Phoenix police officer. If you don't put that gun down, I will kill you where you stand." His voice was different now, calmer, almost sleepy.

Copeland laughed and cocked his head back contemptuously. It was a stupid move.

Before I could even process what was happening, Wolfe had the Chief's Special in his hand and put two rounds between Dennis Copeland's eyes. The small man collapsed backward into the doorway, his fall seeming to take longer than Wolfe's move. Then the loud *crack-crack* faded into a hum in my ears, and a haze of gun smoke sat at eye level like thin morning clouds. I knelt down and confiscated the .44 Magnum.

Wolfe's cold features didn't change. He merely turned and put the gun to Larkin's temple.

Larkin was sweating terribly, and I could see a large stain spreading in the crotch of his pants. He forced his eyes closed and said quietly, "I'll meet you in hell."

Then Wolfe stuck the .38 back in his belt and tossed me a pair of handcuffs.

"You can have him," he said. "I won't give him the satisfaction."

He stepped across Copeland and then turned on the porch.

"You did okay, Mapstone," he said. "Give my regards to Chief Peralta."

Then he walked off into the night.

Susan Knightly greeted me at the door and led me into her condo, an airy, sunlit space of plants and wicker furniture and photographs. On one wall was a moody black-and-white shot of workers in a farm wagon under an ancient oak tree and cloud-scudded sky. "California," she said as I lingered. Inside another simple black metal frame were the faces of two little girls—a color print this time—with old eyes and haunted looks. "The Amazon," she said. We sat on a dark wicker sofa under high windows dense with palm fronds.

"You're a hard man to find," Susan said.

"She said without irony."

She laughed. "Well, I figured after what I read in the paper, it was safe to come out of hiding."

"You hide well."

"Thanks," she said. "I know it seems silly to you, but I was so unnerved by what happened to Phaedra, I didn't know what to do. After that night at the shopping mall, I went to San Francisco for a few days. A friend put me up."

"You could be charged with withholding information in a homicide."

"What?" she laughed. "I told you what I knew. I think you had just promised me protection when the gunfight broke out."

"Okay," I said. "So much for the tough cop routine. You called me. I'm here."

"Look," she said. "Phaedra Riding has caused me more trouble than I would ever have imagined. I was just trying to give her a break."

I watched the palm trees and didn't speak.

"She played the cello, you know," Susan said. "It's a very mournful instrument, when you think about it. I think Phaedra spent most of her life running away from a lot of sadness."

"Sadness with men?" I asked.

"She was a very sensual creature. That part of her set her free from her devils, I think. Maybe only temporarily, and maybe it was self-destructive. But it was enough for a while."

"Love?" I coaxed.

"It wasn't love. Love hurt too much. She told me, 'Always be the one to leave; never be the one who's left.' Quite a philosophy for a twenty-eight-year-old. Once, she told me she always tried to juggle two or three lovers at once so her heart would never be exposed, as she put it. They never knew about one another, of course."

"Sounds like Phaedra had a lot of secrets."

She looked at me with those green eyes. "Haven't you ever had secrets, David? Cheated on your lover? Had a one-night stand with a friend, or with a stranger? Did something you never thought you'd do, and it was strange and wonderful and exciting? You felt alive like you never imagined possible. The next day, you acted like nothing ever happened. That part of your history belongs only to you."

"What I'm after is the secret that will catch a murderer."

We sipped tea and watched a bird fighting to get into the palm tree to nest. She asked, "Why are you here?"

"You called me."

"No, David. I mean, why are you investigating this case? This isn't an unsolved murder case from 1959. Why in the world are you involved in this?"

She had turned the tables on me very neatly. So much for my great interview skills. "It started out personal. Phaedra's sister, Julie, is an old friend of mine from college."

"Talk about secrets," Susan said. "She's an old girlfriend, right?" I nodded. "Men have a way of referring to their old girlfriends. Something in their voices. I've been referred to that way before."

I laughed unhappily. "Julie showed up at my door one night and asked me to see what I could do. I thought I was going to make a phone call and be done with it."

"But you didn't."

"No." I sighed. "No, I stayed with it."

"Why?"

"I can't really say. Something about Phaedra got under my skin. Something mysterious, maybe. Something tragic."

"I think she had that effect on people. She did on me.

"Look," she said, pushing back her hair, "I've been working since I was fourteen years old. Otherwise, God knows what kind of a mess I could have gotten into. I remember when I was Phaedra's age. There's no end to the trouble that can find you . . . especially where men are concerned."

"And you think it was her boyfriend Greg Townsend who got her into the trouble?"

"I never met the man," Susan said. "And Phaedra was afraid to tell me much. But once she got drunk with me and said she had dated a man who flew in cocaine from Mexico. She said she felt like a fool because she didn't even realize it at first; she just thought they were flying to Mexico every other weekend to have a good time."

"But?"

"But something happened. She never told me what. But somehow it became clear to her what Mr. Wonderful was doing. So she told him adios and came back to Phoenix. That's when she went to work for me."

"Did she ever mention somebody named Bobby Hamid?"

She shook her head.

"So what went wrong?"

"I don't know," Susan said. "After she'd been working for me a couple of months, she said one Friday that she was going to Sedona for the weekend. I must have looked at her like, Are you nuts? because she said, 'Susan, don't worry.' That following Monday, she was late, and when she finally came in, she looked like hell. She never seemed the same. About a week after that, she said she had to go away to take care of some business.

"After that, she might call me once a week. I saw her twice. She told me she had overheard something she shouldn't have. She said she was afraid she was going to be killed."

"By whom?" I asked. "By Greg Townsend?"

"She wouldn't say. It was never clear. But as I told you at the mall, she was convinced the cops were paid off and that nobody could be trusted."

"And now Greg's dead, too," I said. "So where does that leave us?"

Susan was silent for a long moment and then said, "I want to show you something."

The sun was nearly gone when I pulled off Grand Avenue into a vast ministorage facility, a rat's maze of low concrete buildings and orange doors. Gang graffiti was splayed across some of the white walls. I drove slowly through the passages until I found two white Ford Crown Victorias sitting bumper-to-bumper, their engines idling. Four detectives got out when I parked and stepped out into the heat.

"John Ford, Glendale Police," said a tall blond man in jeans and work shirt. He nodded to his partner, a short, beefy woman with a sour expression. "Sgt. Carol Quarrels," she said. I showed them my star and ID. All jurisdictional courtesies would be followed.

"You're Mapstone?" This from a member of the second pair, a salt-and-pepper team of sheriff's detectives. I nodded. "We're Kimbrough and Krugell, Sheriff's Homicide, Harquahala task force," the black deputy said. "Got the warrant?"

I pulled out the paper and handed it around. We were in a section of large storage units, accessible through roll-up metal doors. I stared for a moment at the unit I wanted. It had a strong-looking padlock on the door.

"Excuse us for a moment." Kimbrough nodded to me and we walked maybe a dozen paces away from the group. He was tall and handsome, with a shaved head and skin the color of expensive coffee. He looked me over and obviously found me wanting.

"Look," he said. "I don't know who the hell you are, but this is our case. If the sheriff hadn't taken a liking to you for some fucked-up reason, I'd arrest you for interfering in a police investigation. Posse members like you are supposed to ride in parades and help raise money for the sheriff's reelection, and leave the police work to professionals."

"Well, if we find any professionals around here, I'll let you know," I said. He stuck a finger in my chest and gave me a warning look. "And take your goddamned hand off me. I've had a really bad month." I turned away and walked back to the group.

"Let's execute this," I said. "It's hot out here."

Sergeant Quarrels pulled out some bolt cutters, nudged them into the padlock on unit 1663, and snapped the lock off smartly. Her partner slid back the bolt and pulled up the door. Gazing into the gloom inside the storage unit, I could plainly see the dusty hood of a blue Nissan Sentra.

"That's it," I said.

"Call the crime lab. And run that tag," I could hear Kimbrough telling his partner.

We walked in, two on the driver's side, Kimbrough and I on the passenger side, flashlights cutting through the dimness. It smelled of dust and hot concrete and mold.

"Locked this side," said Ford, the male Glendale detective. We shined our lights into the windows and looked through several weeks' worth of dust. "Don't touch anything," Kimbrough told me.

"When did you graduate from the Academy, Kimbrough?" I asked.

"In 1986," he said.

"I graduated in 1979," I said, and walked to the back of the storage unit. Only the car was here. The place was otherwise totally empty, not even trash on the floor. Our steps echoed faintly.

"Why don't we have keys?" Quarrels asked.

I lapsed into cop talk: "Subject stated that victim Riding, who was her employee, left behind only an address for the car, not the keys. Let's pry open that trunk."

"No way," Krugell, the other sheriff's dick, said behind me. "We're waiting for the evidence techs. Tag comes back to the victim, Phaedra Riding."

I glanced at Kimbrough and shrugged.

Kimbrough looked at me for a moment and then pulled two pairs of latex gloves from his pocket, handing me one pair. "Go get a crowbar," he said to his partner.

In a moment, Krugell came back with a crowbar.

We were all really sweating now. My hands felt especially strange inside the latex in such heat. I grasped the crowbar under the trunk latch and jammed it in deep. Then I leaned down. At first, the lock held, fought me. Then there was a *pop* sound and the trunk lid came up. Flashlight beams converged on black athletic bags laid neatly side by side. I pulled out an Uzi and handed it to Kimbrough.

"Always be prepared," he said, checking the action. "Loaded, full magazine."

"I'm opening one of the bags," I said, finding a zipper and pulling it toward me. Even before I opened the bag all the way, I could see the bundled stacks of hundred-dollar bills inside.

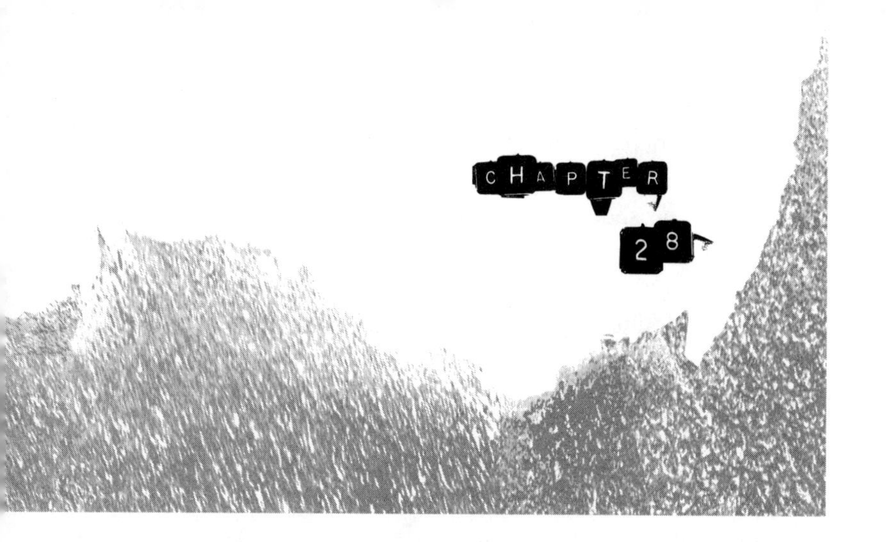

Peralta's black Ford swept into the narrow passageway nearly an hour later, a red light rotating lazily on the dash, reflecting off the orange doors all around us. The sun was all the way down, and the Crime Scene Unit guys had set up floodlights around the storage unit, which only made things hotter, if that was possible. The big man shook hands with the Glendale officers and then walked over to us, losing his smile.

"This is not one of the Harquahala ones, Chief," Krugell said. "Phaedra Riding is not one of our serial victims."

"What, Krugell, do I look like a moron?" Peralta said. "I've known that for days." That was news to me. He looked over me and Kimbrough. "Well? Any new gunfights involving 1950s homicide investigations tonight?" It was asked without humor.

"No, but we have three bags full of money," I said. "I always knew I'd get rich off the SO."

Peralta snorted. "How much?"

"Rough guesstimate, a million, million two," Kimbrough said. "We haven't had time to count it."

"I should have known our 'Phaedra like Phoenix' was running dope if she wasn't turning tricks," Peralta said.

"We don't know that, Mike."

"I really think you have a thing for this girl, Mapstone," he said. "Too bad the department shrinks don't work with part-time deputies." He looked over the car.

"Prints," he shouted. "I want prints." The evidence technicians put their heads down and dusted.

"So it's drug money?" he asked.

"Lindsey found the DEA file on Greg Townsend. He was Phaedra's boyfriend. Rich boy, part-time pilot. And, according to confidential informants, he was a mule for Bobby Hamid, flying in cocaine from Mexico."

Peralta's jaw tightened. "Bobby fucking Hamid. I should have known he'd eventually turn up. Who is Lindsey, and why is she looking at DEA files?" He looked at me. "Never mind. Jesus, were you this much trouble when you were a history professor?"

"Probably worse," Kimbrough said, but the edge was gone from his voice.

I asked, "Have we checked in with Coconino County on the progress of their investigation of Townsend's murder?"

Everybody was silent.

"What's so hard about this?" said Kimbrough's partner. "Chick and boyfriend are supposed to carry the cash down to Mexico and bring back cocaine, whatever. Instead, they keep the cash, rip off Bobby Hamid, hide the car here, and wait for the heat to cool down. Bobby finds 'em first, kills 'em both." He made pistols out of his fingers. *Pop. Pop.*

Peralta and Kimbrough looked at me.

"Doesn't make sense," I said. "Phaedra was plainly on the run. But if Greg Townsend was, too, why was he waiting at home in Sedona when I found him?"

" 'Cause mules are stupid," Kimbrough said.

"This guy wasn't stupid," I said. "Ignorant, perhaps, but not stupid. And a million bucks is a lot for a mule to be entrusted with, don't you think? And Phaedra hated drugs. Everybody says that. And why would Bobby Hamid leave Phaedra's body where it would be immediately found, posed like Rebecca Stokes's was?"

Peralta pulled out a handkerchief and wiped his brow. "So what do we know? Tell me what we know."

"We know she was on the run for approximately a month, most of the time living with her new boyfriend, Noah. She kept in sporadic touch with Susan Knightly, her boss, who said Phaedra admitted to overhearing something she shouldn't have, something she was afraid of."

I added, "And we know she met her sister at a coffee place in Tempe the night before her body turned up."

There was a long, awful pause. "I want her," Peralta snapped. "I want Julie Riding."

I started to say something, but I thought, Why? What argument can I make? What argument would I want to make? God, I felt tired.

"And," Kimbrough said, "we know Phaedra's car was hidden in this storage unit with a million dollars and a machine gun in the trunk. If that doesn't tie Phaedra to the deal, I don't know what does."

"Noah—that's the latest boyfriend—said Phaedra was without a car, that her sister had borrowed it," I announced.

"Jesus!" Peralta shouted. "I want this bitch in jail by morning! Why didn't I arrest her that first day?"

"Mike . . ."

He stabbed a thick finger at me. "Goddamn it, David, if you know where she is, you'd better have her booked into the women's unit by the next time I see you. Do you hear me? If you go thinking with your johnson on this, you're going to be in a world of hurt."

Fifteen faces looked up at me. I started to say something, but Peralta cut me off. "I want her in jail. Got it? You wanted to be on this case. Well, consider yourself on it. I want Julie Riding."

He walked to his car, shouting as he went. "I want Julie Riding in jail. I want those prints. Fibers, mud, semen, anything in that car. I want that cash inventoried and locked up. I want that car impounded and torn apart. I want the paperwork on this storage unit. And I want Bobby Hamid down at Madison Street tomorrow morning with that high-priced mouthpiece of his."

He climbed in his Ford, slammed the door, and gunned the engine, disappearing around the corner of the rat's maze, trailing exhaust fumes and dust.

Where was Dr. Sharon when I needed her?

"I have to warn you, Peralta, this is the most egregious case of police harassment I've seen in all my years of practicing law. What you have here isn't a case. It's a fantasy."

For an hour, we were crammed into a Spartan white-walled interrogation room: Peralta and me, Bobby Hamid and his lawyer. More detectives were listening behind the one-way glass. The man speaking was the lawyer, Bruton Hennessey, an intense, short, florid-faced easterner who had migrated to Arizona two decades ago and made a name defending high-paying dirtbags.

While Hennessey and Peralta jousted, I was watching Bobby Hamid. He was about my height but more slender, wrapped in a gray suit of the texture and cut that doesn't even start below a thousand dollars, all set off by a subtle blue Hermès tie. He was the epitome of swarthy meets money: his darkness offset by delicate features, brooding, feminine eyes, and an expensive haircut and manicure. He had walked into the room, shaken our hands—to Peralta's visible distress—and let lawyer Hennessey do the talking.

"I mean, really, Peralta, do you have nothing better to do than try to hang the flimsiest charges on my client, a businessman responsible for no small amount of taxes in this county? . . ."

Peralta snarled, "Cut the shit, Hennessey. This ain't Boston. If I had a dollar for every illegal activity the Ayatollah here was involved with, I'd be a rich man."

"Chief Peralta," Bobby Hamid said. "There is no need for your anti-Persian bigotry. Anyway, I am an Episcopalian; we have no ayatollahs."

Peralta stood and leaned over Bobby Hamid's chair. I imagined what he'd do if the lawyer wasn't there. Instead, he said, "Greg Townsend. He was a business associate of yours, I believe?"

"I don't know the name," Bobby Hamid said.

"Townsend was a pilot and his phone records show repeated calls during the month of June from his Sedona home to Tiffany's, a topless bar on Van Buren where you are known to receive business calls," I said. Lindsey had come through again.

"He was flying in cocaine," Peralta said. "And now he's dead and tied to a million dollars left in the back of a car. Somebody used a twelve-gauge shotgun to paint the walls of his bedroom. Meanwhile, his girlfriend turned up in the desert, raped and strangled. It's murder, and it's got your name all over it, Bobby."

Hennessey said, "Mr. Hamid doesn't have to answer any of this, Peralta. If you have a case, charge him. I'll have him out in two hours."

"Bruton, please." Bobby Hamid put a manicured hand on the lawyer's arm. "I have nothing to hide. I was in Aspen during the time you say this Townsend fellow and his girlfriend were killed, and Bruton here can produce the documentation and witnesses. I honestly didn't know them. I'm sorry they're dead, truly I am. But I'm afraid I can't help you."

He smiled at Peralta. "You know, the illegal drug business is very dangerous, I hear."

"We found a million dollars in the trunk of a car in Glendale," Peralta said. "If somebody stole a million dollars from me, I'd be tempted to use a twelve-gauge on him. I wouldn't want to get a reputation in the drug business as somebody you could rip off with impunity."

"That's because you are a brutal man, Chief Peralta." Hamid smiled.

"The phone calls?" Peralta demanded.

"Come, come, Chief. That club is a little tax write-off for me, one of three dozen enterprises I own. Are you really expecting me to know who calls every business? That would be a little like expecting Bill Gates to know every call that comes into Microsoft, no?"

"If Microsoft sold cocaine," Peralta muttered.

Bobby Hamid continued: "Why, your pilot was probably calling because he had a crush on one of the girls." He laughed, and so did Hennessey. Peralta looked at me. We had shot our wad, and it wasn't much.

"Do you remember a young woman named Phaedra?" I asked.

"Phaedra." Bobby Hamid studied his cuticle. "In Greek mythology, she was the daughter of Minos. Met a bad end, as I recall."

"Hey, raghead!" Peralta shouted, "this ain't Western Civ one oh one. Do you know a twenty-eight-year-old woman named Phaedra Riding? Red hair, pretty."

Something flickered in his eyes. He smiled sadly at Peralta. "I don't know any Phaedra Riley."

Shut up in his office, Peralta was momentarily serene.

"Bobby's one of the many things that have changed about the Valley since you left," he said, sitting behind his desk, twirling in his chair, mashing a stressball in his massive hand. "Changed for the worse. At least we put Charlie Keating in prison for awhile."

"Bobby knows about Townsend," I said.

Peralta nodded. "The sheer size of the cash we found points to a major player like Bobby. And the CI report on Townsend makes it even more likely. But I don't have enough to take to the county attorney. It would be a waste of the taxpayers' money. Someday, Bobby will get careless, and when that happens, I'm gonna see they lock him up for the next thousand years."

I asked about Phaedra's car, and he pointed to a file folder on the corner of his desktop. I opened it and read.

"Dirt and cholla spines on the carpet on the driver's side," I said aloud. "Consistent with the soil and vegetation of the murder scene?"

Peralta nodded.

"The ministorage lease is in the name of Jamie Johnson. Three nine seven seven East Bethany Home Road?"

"It's a fake name and fake address. The clerk who rented it left the company, and we can't find him to ask what the person looked like, or even whether they were female or male."

I was reading on. "Prints."

"Lots of Phaedra's," Peralta said. "Electrostatic gear picked up some others. But it could be weeks before we get anywhere on that. It could be never."

"So, we think the car might have been driven out to the desert, maybe to do the body drop. But otherwise, we're basically nowhere."

"Not necessarily," Peralta said. "Where is Julie?"

I sat down in front of the desk and shrugged. "We checked her apartment, her ex-husband. Nothing so far."

"Has she called you again?"

"Not for a few days, not since the last call I told you about."

"She'll call," Peralta said. This was the cool, shrewd Peralta. All the anger from the day before was gone. I wondered if he even remembered it.

"Do you really believe Julie is involved in this?"

"You believe it, too," he said simply. "I don't know exactly how. But she knows a hell of a lot more than she's told us so far."

"I can't believe Julie would murder her own sister."

Peralta exhaled heavily. "My mother and her oldest sister didn't speak for thirty years. I can believe it. But she sure as hell didn't rape Phaedra. If Julie's involved, someone else is, too. A guy."

He stood up and put on his Stetson. "We're raiding a militia training ground up by Saguaro Lake. Want to come? You haven't been shot at in at least two days."

I reached across his desk, opened his humidor, and took a couple of cigars. "No thanks. I've got work to do."

The vast west side of Phoenix has none of the glamour of Scottsdale and Paradise Valley. It lacks even the natural beauty of Camelback and the other mountains to the east. It's as flat as Nebraska. Not too may years ago, it was just miles and miles of fields: cotton, lettuce, cabbage, alfalfa. Open irrigation ditches shaded by cottonwood trees ran on either side of two-lane farm roads, marking every mile like a precise checkerboard. Only Grand Avenue sliced crosswise through the checkerboard, heading northwest through a little railroad town called Glendale, where Mexican men in straw hats iced the refrigerator cars to carry Arizona produce east.

Now, it's all houses and strip shopping and malls. The ditches and cottonwoods are gone, and the former farm roads can't be widened fast enough: six lanes, eight lanes. Glendale is a city in its own right—population 200,000—and the tiny farm hamlets like Peoria, Youngtown and El Mirage are full-blown suburbs. And Sun City, with its lazy, curving wide streets and golf courses and neat desert-landscaped haciendas baking in the sun.

When the first Sun City subdivisions were cut into the lettuce fields in the early 1960s, someone asked Grandmother if she would be moving out there. "No," she said. "I don't want to live around all those old people." But tens of thousands of other folks weren't like

Grandmother—especially retirees from Cleveland and Rochester and Detroit who couldn't bear the thought of another brutal winter—and now Sun City has a settled, almost crowded look that would have seemed impossible thirty years ago.

But "the active lifestyle" was still for sale here: Golf carts piddled up and down the spotless streets. Every few blocks held some kind of activity center, promising summer painting classes, swimming lessons, and, for the adventurous, martial arts and rock climbing. A couple of hardy souls were speed walking in the 110-degree broiler, past a sign discreetly promoting the Sun City Symphony's summer season. A Sheriff's Office patrol car sped past me, going in the opposite direction: maybe to a heart attack, maybe to a murder.

Dr. Sharon was on the radio—her show was addictive—lecturing some tremulous-voiced bag of emotions about "woulda, coulda, shoulda." "Stop that!" she commanded in that voice that had attitude but somehow never made anybody mad. I thought, Shoulda known something was wrong with Julie; woulda worked harder to find Phaedra if I'd known she was in trouble; coulda seen the Stokes case would lead to trouble. Stop that, I said to myself. I turned off Del Webb Boulevard at 105th Avenue and parked in front of the single-story home of Avis Riding, Julie's mother.

I knocked four times on the aluminum screen door before I heard a little dog barking and sensed someone looking out through the peephole of the main door. I held up my ID card. More barking. Then: "Please go away. I've answered questions until I just can't talk anymore."

"Mrs. Riding, it's David Mapstone."

The dog started in again. I momentarily considered shooting the .357 Python through the door at dog level just to get some peace.

"Julie and I dated when we were at ASU."

"I remember you." She was there suddenly, the door opening quickly. She was smaller than I recalled, with hair the color of winter straw. She was wearing a white top and light blue shorts, and her skin was that leathery brown that comes from too many years in the Arizona sun. She regarded me with puffy eyes.

"I thought you were some kind of a teacher now."

"I'm working with the Sheriff's Office again," I said over the barking. "I'm very sorry to bother you at a time like this, but it's important."

"Wait." She carried the little dog away, and I heard a door shut somewhere in the back of the house. She came back and invited me in. While she led me into a living room drowning in the smell of potpourri and wet dog, I went through the essentials, saying how sorry I was about Phaedra, how Julie had come to me, asking me to help find her sister, and how I now needed to find Julie.

"Do you have children?" she asked in a voice that sounded like it hurt even to speak.

I told her I didn't.

"Then you'll never know," she said. "You'll never know what it's like to lose your child, to outlive your child." My eyes went to a large high school graduation photo of Phaedra on the wall.

Mrs. Riding avoided it, staring out into the backyard, a sunny, narrow space with a neat Bermuda grass lawn and low hedges.

"Julie and I aren't close. We never have been, and we've hardly spoken the past three years. I don't have any idea where she is. Why?"

"I think she knows something about what happened to Phaedra."

I expected some reaction, but she continued in the same monotone. "I knew something like this would happen someday. I knew if Phaedra kept trying to help Julie, I'd end up losing both of them."

"Mrs. Riding, I got the impression it was the other way around, that Julie was trying to help Phaedra."

She snorted an unhappy laugh. "Julie was never sober enough to help anybody but herself, even if she would have been inclined. That's what lost her her daughter. And it's a good thing."

"And you have no idea where she might be?"

She shook her head slowly. "Julie ran with a fast crowd," she said. "Money, parties, powerful men. But it was all going to catch up with her. She couldn't keep her looks forever." She looked from the lawn to me. "She was so much like her father. She was her father's daughter. Phaedra was my daughter." Her voice skipped a bit, like a stone skimming water. "My hope."

"I thought Julie and her father didn't get along."

"They hated each other," she said, "because they were the same. Do you want something to drink?"

I said a diet Coke would be nice, and she brought me one. She poured herself Jack Daniel's on the rocks.

"Both my daughters were very complicated, very smart young women. But Julie, Julie had something in her, something like what was in her father. It was something that you could never know, that made it possible for her to do things I could never do."

"I've decided we never really know the people we're close to," I ventured.

"Maybe," Avis Riding said. "Maybe so. I know that my husband—" She stopped herself. "That's not the entire truth. I know we both did things that made life harder, more painful for the girls. Well, isn't that what we're supposed to believe? That whatever happened to Julie and Phaedra was ultimately the parents' fault? That's what all those women who call Dr. Sharon on the radio say."

"I don't think Sharon agrees with them," I said.

"I don't know what I think," she said. "I know I was married to a cold, angry man with too many secrets, and it somehow seemed to bring out the worst in me, too."

"What was Phaedra's relationship with Julie?"

"Complicated. Phaedra was very strong, very independent. But she loved Julie unquestioningly, and so many times, Phaedra was there to get her out of a bad love affair, get her into detox for the cocaine."

"You stayed in touch with Phaedra?"

She nodded.

"What about the month before her death?"

"She'd call. She seemed worried, didn't want to talk. I told all this to those other men, the black detective and that annoying partner of his. I didn't know she was in danger."

"Did Julie call you in the past month?"

"Yes, she did," she said. "It was probably the first time we'd even spoken in months."

"What did you talk about?"

"She wanted to know where Phaedra was."

"What did you tell her?"

"I told her if she wasn't at her apartment, she could call Phaedra's new boyfriend. Noah was his name. Do you want the number?"

"No," I said a little too quietly, and then said I had to leave.

"Wait," she said. "I'm a little surprised you don't have a family of your own by now. You seemed like a nice boy."

I smiled a little. "Life doesn't work out like we expect."

"I don't mean to go on like a lonely old woman. I just haven't talked to a soul for days, except the police. And I know you are the police, but you're also someone I know."

"I thought you never liked me."

She spread her hands. "Oh, those were hard times. I know Julie used to bring you over to dinner to keep the peace, knowing with an outsider we'd all behave ourselves." She smiled just a little. "I knew. But you were the only boy Julie ever brought home who seemed to have some substance to him. A little intimidating perhaps, but smart as a whip."

I mumbled some thanks.

"I always loved to read, you know. That's where I found Phaedra's name. I always loved that name. I tried to instill that love of learning in my girls." She looked me over for the first time. "You're how old, David?"

"I'm forty."

"I remember that time so well," she said. "Everything will change for you now. I don't mean you'll buy a sports car and run off with a blonde. But over the next few years, things will change. I don't know if it will be for the better. But maybe you can lose some of that anger and pain that's inside you."

I started to say something, but she smiled again. "Once upon a time, I thought you might be my son-in-law. I didn't know what the hell we'd talk about, but I knew you and Julie would make smart children. It's so funny the way life turns out."

* * *

Outside, I thought of Avis Riding's words: "It's so funny the way life turns out." I leaned against the side of the Blazer and cut and lighted one of Peralta's cigars. So funny. I remembered the rages Julie would have about her father. I remembered the way she would cling to me in the night, when sleep took away her hatred and left her with nothing but fear. I am forty years old, I mused, and I honestly can't say how I got to this point. My peers now have teenage children and careers and settled marriages and graying hair and maybe, maybe a sense of place, a truce with the dreams we have to give up, most of us anyway. I'm just me, here. The way things turn out. Funny.

As I drew the tobacco across my palate and felt sorry for myself, a cruiser slowly crept down the street and stopped by me. The shift snapped into park. The window came down. "You have business on this block, sir?" the deputy asked, her hand obviously down at her holster.

I handed her the wallet with my star and ID.

"Sorry," she said. "Mapstone." Then she lowered her sunglasses a bit and smiled—a nice smile. "Hey, you're the history guy."

Yeah, I'm the history guy.

I reached Sedona a little after 3:00 P.M., and was able to throttle back the air-conditioning, being more than three thousand feet above the desert floor that holds Phoenix. Every few miles were signs warning about the high fire danger—the biggest reminder being the plume of smoke on the northwest edge of the Verde Valley, which the radio said was part of the wildfires that had consumed a million acres of forests in the West this summer. A million acres of fire. A million dollars in the trunk of Phaedra's car.

I had lunch at a Mexican place on the Tlaquepaque, the town square near Oak Creek. I fortified myself with two Negra Modelos, a beer that tastes incredibly sublime when consumed with a plate of enchiladas in a dark, cool, adobe-protected space. Then I walked over to the Coconino County Sheriff's Substation and asked for Deputy Allison Taylor. She was about my age, with light brown hair the style and texture of Lauren Hutton's and a very large Magnum on her hip.

"David Mapstone of the MCSO," she said, extending a tanned, slender hand. "I'm impressed."

"Oh, no."

"You've made it respectable to be a deputy sheriff *and* be intelligent."

I cocked an eyebrow.

"I studied premed at Wake Forest," she said, leading me back to a squad room cluttered with desks, paperwork, and a large, ancient fax machine. "Then I made my first trip west and decided I didn't want to be a doctor after all."

"Life plays those funny tricks on us," I said.

"And I take it you don't want to teach college anymore?"

"I wouldn't say that. I love writing and teaching. I just can't get a job."

"Marry a millionaire, that's my advice."

"Tried it. Didn't work."

She made an exaggerated O with her mouth. I liked her.

"So you want the Townsend case," she said, fishing in a file cabinet.

"We think it might be tied to another homicide down in the Valley."

"What a big ugly city down there," she said. "L.A. two. 'Course, I'm a small-town girl." She handed over a sheaf of papers and photographs.

"Not too many cases like that around here," Allison said. "We have a permanent population in Oak Creek Canyon of about fifteen thousand. But with three million visitors a year, we get our share of crime and nuttiness. Hell, with four vortexes—to channel New Age Vibes—we get more than our share of nuttiness."

"Any leads?"

"Seems execution-style," she said. "Very ugly, though. This asshole made him put the barrel of the shotgun in his mouth and then pulled the trigger. What a mess." My own mouth ached. "We hear you guys tied him into drug trafficking?"

I told her about the DEA report and Bobby Hamid.

"Well, there's certainly an appetite for cocaine up here," she said. "Wherever the beautiful people congregate, there's that. What's the saying? Cocaine is God's way of letting you know you have too much money."

We laughed, and I asked if she'd ever run across Townsend.

"No," she said. "That's a very exclusive part of the canyon. And very remote."

"So the neighbors didn't hear or see anything?"

She shook her head. "People with money like you find here don't want embarrassing police investigations interrupting their lives. We're supposed to keep the traffic manageable, drag off the worst fruitcakes, and keep burglars away from the art galleries. They don't want to entertain the notion that their nice neighbor might have been a dirtbag. And we're a small department, with not many people or much money. If you guys can help, go to it."

"Autopsy?" I asked, leafing through the report.

"Still tied up in Phoenix," she said. "It takes longer and longer to get reports back now that there are more and more exotic tests to perform."

I sat down to read.

"You know," she said, "there's a lot about this case that's screwy. He had a very expensive alarm system out there, and it was fully engaged when the first deputy arrived after the murder."

Forty-five minutes later, I was on the winding road up into the red rocks, through firs and ponderosa pines, up to Greg Townsend's million-dollar house. It wasn't a day very different from the first time I was here. This time, I found the place deserted, with a Sheriff's Department NO TRESPASSING seal on the door. I used the keys given me by Allison Taylor to disengage the alarm and let myself in.

The house was still immaculate and spectacular, but there's something about a place that has been violated by murder: a smell real or imagined, brutal memories in the walls, uneasy ghosts. Lindsey had offered to take the day off and come up with me, and I found myself wishing she were here. I picked up the phone and called down to Phoenix, getting her voice mail. I left a message and remembered how she'd felt in bed just hours earlier.

Although it's commonplace today to read nothing more than the TV screen, it still jarred me to see no books. But it went with the expensively austere theme of the decorator. I looked over the photos on his shelves and noted once again that there were no photos of him and Phaedra. There were pictures of him with other women, kayaking, on the beach, rock climbing, in the cockpit of a small airplane. I had definitely lived too sedentary a life.

The master bedroom had been stripped of furniture, but the walls were still stained with blood—lots of it. I stepped inside. The bed must have faced the door. He would have seen his assailant coming, if he had been awake, if he had been expecting trouble. It was so quiet, I jumped when the phone began to ring. When no answering machine picked up, I lifted the receiver and placed it to my ear. Whoever was on the other end hung up, saying nothing.

Townsend had been very neat, precise. So, too, had his murderer. Nothing was out of place in the office. Even the stunning Navajo rug that dominated the room was hung with obsessive care on the wall. I sat at his desk, tried not to let the view of Oak Creek Canyon distract me, and went through the drawers. Bills, blank stationery, a checkbook, some computer disks that I fed into the IBM clone nearby, which yielded holistic healing techniques, FAA flight-plan regulations, some computer games, maps of the fourteen-thousand-foot peaks in Colorado. I was not finding that "I am a drug dealer" file. Then I reached under the computer table and felt a slender journal taped to the underside. Life was getting interesting.

It was full of columns of numbers and letters, a code of some kind. Pages and pages of it in a simple binder, noted in a precise hand in black ink, always black ink. Maybe it had something to do with Sedona's psychic voltage. Or maybe it tracked drug shipments and payments for Bobby Hamid. I took it with me and walked back to the Blazer.

I walked around the grounds, hoping for footprints, shotgun shells, Baggies of dope, signed confessions. I wasn't proud at this stage. The place was so remote, clinging as it did to the side of the mountain, it was easy to see why no one would have seen anything. Through the pines, I could see little but hillside, while at my back was the blue of the canyon sky. It was a fabulous place, a "babe lair," as my male students would have said, a place sure to have impressed a young woman who was attracted to the quirky, the beautiful, and the expensive.

In a clearing, someone had laid out a medicine wheel in the red dirt. Some Indian tribes used them for their spiritual powers, but they had been co-opted by the New Agers. This one was probably fake, but it did make me look in a certain direction. Something glinted at me from an outcropping about fifty yards above, up the mountainside. I negotiated some boulders and climbed, pulling myself up on fir branches, crossing a fallen aspen trunk. The rocks and soil were the color of the sunset and covered with pine needles. My legs were feeling the angle of the climb by the time I pulled myself up on the ledge and found a door.

A door. And a cabin. There was an adobe wall maybe twenty feet across, set neatly into the rock. The cabin was obviously fairly new and had a commanding view of Greg Townsend's house and the canyon and forest reaching below and off to the horizon. Yet from even a few feet below, it was nearly invisible. I was preparing to show my star and knock on the door, when it opened and there stood Julie.

"David, I hoped you wouldn't come up here."

Julie walked back inside the cabin, and I followed her. It was a foolhardy thing to do. But I was feeling foolhardy. Homer tells of how the Greek soldiers before Troy lost their senses and became drunk for war. I suppose it was that way for me, only I was drunk with a kind of flinty curiosity—I had to know; I had to *know.*

"I keep wondering what you said to Phaedra the night before she died," I said. "When you met her at the coffee shop on Mill Avenue. What you said that upset her so much."

Julie twirled a strand of hair and looked out the window.

"You ask too many questions, David."

"I suspect she didn't really realize what she was into even at the end," I went on. "She was gentle and trusting and too eccentric."

"You were always such a sentimental sap," Julie said. "Phaedra was a little moralizing bitch sometimes, but she knew the color of money."

"Even if it was money that belonged to Bobby Hamid?"

"I don't know who it really belonged to, but it's mine now," she said. "I earned it. More money than you can imagine."

"So that's what you meant about us being in grave danger?"

Julie was silent.

"What about Phaedra? Did she realize she was in danger?"

"You don't want to go there, David."

"Oh, but I do. I am there."

She sighed and looked at me like some pathetic being. "No money, no life. It's that simple."

"So Greg decided to rip off his employer?"

"Not Greg," Julie said. "Give me more credit than that."

I arched an eyebrow.

"I wasn't going to spend the rest of my life working, watching the beautiful life go on all around me." Her voice rose. "Jesus! All I had to do was walk around to see everything I couldn't have. Do you have any idea how hard it is to be broke in Phoenix?"

"So a million dollars in cocaine money was the ticket? You just thought you'd stay in town and everything would be fine?"

"That was the plan," she said.

"The plan where Greg Townsend and Phaedra took the fall? And Julie is left with the money?" I felt an overpowering revulsion.

"Nobody's innocent. Everybody got what they wanted."

"Really?" I said. "Everyone I talked to said Phaedra hated drugs. So what did she get?"

"She got stupid. She got in the way."

"She was your sister."

Julie clenched and unclenched her hands, but she was silent.

"So Phaedra didn't know about the drugs or the money?"

"Not at first," Julie said.

"But she overheard."

Julie said, "All she had to do was be her weird, ethereal self. Always missing half the world right in front of her nose. That's all she had to do. And nothing would have happened."

"But it didn't work out that way. Phaedra heard about ripping off Bobby Hamid, taking his money and failing to deliver the product. She got scared and she ran. She stayed on the run for over a month. Were you really afraid she'd narc on you?"

"There's more to it than that," Julie said.

"So eventually, you found her. You found her, and you told her something that persuaded her to meet you, and then to follow you away from a public place. The next thing you know, she's dead in the desert."

"I didn't hurt her," Julie said, her left eye twitching. "I couldn't."

"But you found her. And she couldn't be allowed to live, knowing what she knew."

There was an odd brightness in her eyes. "I had to have the money. I didn't have any chances left. You don't understand. With the money, I could have a life; I could get Mindy back."

"And buy more cocaine."

She let out some breath.

"So where did I come in?"

"You?" She sounded disoriented.

"You came to me, remember? You asked me to look into Phaedra's disappearance? Then you cried when I told you I'd done all I could do. So I jumped into it, up to my eyeballs."

"You always had a 'white knight' fantasy," she said. "I knew you couldn't resist."

"So you had it planned from the start. When Phaedra ran, you hoped I could help you find her. And that I could also be your cover. Your old boyfriend, who worked with the Sheriff's Office, could muck around and draw attention away from the person who really killed Phaedra. And then I was the perfect alibi: I was the one who saw you cry at the Phoenician when I told you about Phaedra. I was the one who defended you in front of Peralta and the detectives."

She lit a cigarette. "You give me too much credit, David. I was scared. I didn't know what to do."

"I imagine your sister was scared, too."

She was silent for a long moment. Suddenly, her eyes filled with tears. "I never meant for her to get hurt."

"Oh, cut the shit, Julie," I said sharply. "Turn it off. I've wised up about you, finally. I know about your cocaine habit. I know you had Phaedra's car. I know you were with her the night before she was found murdered. It was all a lie: that you hadn't seen her for weeks, that you didn't know why she'd disappeared. And everything about us was a lie, too."

"You never knew me," she said, crying now. "You never knew how awful it was growing up. How my mother never gave me—"

I cut her off. "This isn't about you anymore, Julie. This is about Phaedra's murder."

She looked at me oddly. "What are you talking about?"

I grabbed her and shook her hard. "I'm talking about your little sister, Phaedra. She had red hair and played the cello and was afraid to fall in love. Somebody raped her and strangled her and left her in the desert, trying to make it look like a copycat killing, a link to a 1950s murder. Why, Julie? Why?"

Julie dropped the cigarette, grabbed my arms, and dug her nails into them. She looked at me with something wild in her eyes and crumpled slowly to the floor, shaking, hyperventilating. She wailed, "Noooooooooooo. Noooooooooooooooo. Noooooooooooo."

I pulled her up off the floor, a limp doll. "Stop the acting, Julie. We're going to Phoenix."

The voice behind me said, "She's not acting."

I turned and was looking at Greg Townsend.

"And of course nobody's going to Phoenix."

He had a pistol in his right hand, pointed at my chest.

"She has these breaks," Greg Townsend said. Julie was on the floor, grasping my trouser leg, sobbing uncontrollably. "I don't know if the drugs do this to her or if it's more." He was damned chatty for a man who had a pistol trained on me.

"I'll have that gun," he said, indicating the Python. He took a step toward me, thought better of getting too close, and backed up a step. "Put it on the floor."

About five feet separated me from Townsend and the small black automatic he was holding. And that became my world, a small, hard place to live.

"The gun!" he said sharply.

"I don't think so," I said. Old training is supposed to kick in at such times. I don't know if that was what happened. I just remembered Peralta's first axiom: "Never give up your gun."

"Are you out of your mind?"

"Nobody gets my gun," I said, trying not to let my voice shake. "You're going to kill me anyway, so I may as well take you down with me."

Now his hand shook a little, and he took a step backward. "I've got the drop on you, pig. You're not taking me anywhere. I'm telling you for the last time, drop your gun!"

"You have the drop on me with a small-caliber weapon. You can shoot it and kill me. But I'll still be able to pull out this very large-caliber revolver and put three or four hollow points into your sorry ass." It was bravado I didn't even believe, but I was committed now. No turning back. If my heart had beat any faster, it would have exploded.

He said, "Why the fuck are you here, Mapstone? I thought we were rid of you."

"You never should have brought me into this in the first place."

"That was her." He indicated Julie. "She can be quite clever when she's lucid."

"And what about you? Back from the dead?"

He smiled. "It worked. As far as that prick Bobby knows, I'm dead and his money is long gone."

"That's not showing much gratitude for a man who seems to have set you up pretty damned well," I said.

"Entrepreneurship is the American dream," Townsend said. "I was tired of working for someone else. And when you work for Bobby, the run is great, but it always ends. I knew it was coming to an end. I handled the high-end shipments, the big money, and the risks were just too great. Bobby would have given me up to DEA and written it off as a tax deduction. But with a million dollars in seed money and the right clients, I'd turn old Bobby over to the feds and take his business."

"So who died in your place?"

He looked annoyed. "Some drifter Julie picked up down in town. We had a few drinks, found out he had no one to miss him, and in general, he did have my body type." Townsend laughed. "Julie told him we wanted him to join a threesome."

"You took a chance that the cops would assume it was you."

"Cops get busy like everybody else," he said. "I wanted to make this easy for them. After I had the money stashed away, I set up our drifter to look like me. I knew the cops had intelligence linking me to Bobby Hamid, so they'd assume it was a drug execution. Then I had this place, secluded, but I could watch the comings and goings down below. First the cops. Then Bobby's people, twice. It was like 'hide in plain sight.' They never knew I was here."

"It almost worked," I said. "But when you start murdering people, it's hard to make things go right."

He looked at me.

"Phaedra. She had someone who would miss her and find out what happened. And that was me."

"Very commendable, Professor Mapstone," Townsend said. "And you are going to get the chance to join her, if you believe in the oppressive bullshit doctrines of Christianity and Western civilization."

"Well then, we'll both head that way." I put my hand on the Python's grip.

"I didn't hurt her," said Julie, who sat back on the floor between us, rocking back and forth, running her fingers through her hair. "I just needed the money."

"Shut up, Julie," he said sharply, watching her and then me.

"You shut up!" she screamed. "You told me this morning you loved me and that we'd finally get married."

"Bitch," he said.

I said, "I guess I should have known from the start that she was yours."

"Oh, and how's that?"

"She had bad taste in men," I said. "And it didn't add up that you and Phaedra got together through the personals. That would be a risk for someone in your, uh, profession. You met Phaedra because you were already involved with her big sister. That must have been complicated."

"You can't stop, can you?" Townsend said, gripping the gun tighter. "You just have to know what happened."

"And why."

"Is that the historian in you, or the cop?" he sneered. "A famous man said, 'History is mostly bunk.' "

"Henry Ford," I said. "He also admired Adolf Hitler."

Townsend shook his head, smiled, and indicated Julie. "We first met on the party circuit in Phoenix. Julie was with some dickhead lawyer who liked to get her fucked up on cocaine. We hit it off. You can understand, I'm sure. You two were an item in college, right? But Phaedra was, like, in bloom. First time I saw her, I knew I had to do whatever it took."

"Like concealing the fact that you were a drug mule."

"It's a big business, Mapstone, and I made more money in a week than you'll make in a lifetime."

"But not enough to ensure 'happily ever after' with Phaedra."

"Julie wouldn't leave it alone, wouldn't stay away. One morning, she caught me and Phaedra in bed and tried to kill us both with a butcher knife. It was bad news. Phaedra left and went back to Phoenix."

"So why couldn't you leave her out of it? If she didn't know you were into drugs, why did she have to know that you were going to rip off Bobby Hamid for a million dollars?"

"My fault," he said breezily. "I wanted Phaedra in my life. She had a real hold on me sexually. But Julie was my lover and my business partner. I needed them both."

I arched an eyebrow.

"Julie was a pipeline for some very high-powered people in North Phoenix and Scottsdale society. You think those people come home and have a martini? Cocaine is the drug of choice, and Julie—from her days as a piece of expensive eye candy—knew the right people. If I was going to supplant Bobby Hamid, I had to have Julie."

"So," I said, "you got Phaedra to come back for the weekend. I guess Julie was supposed to be gone. She came back unexpectedly, and you quarreled. She threatened to go to Bobby Hamid about your plans, and Phaedra overheard. So Phaedra took off, and you had to go find her. Am I close?"

"Very close, Professor Mapstone," Townsend said. "I am impressed. If you must know, there was also something specific that Phaedra knew—a place I use to store things—and I couldn't take a chance with her knowing that."

Julie had been silently crying through all this, but suddenly she said, "I told him just to let her go. She wouldn't bother us. She was already disgusted with both of us and wanted to be as far away from this as she could get."

"Shut the fuck up, Julie," he snarled. "You wanted the money as badly as I did."

"And you came to me to find Phaedra," I said. "So you must have had something in mind."

"I knew you'd protect her," Julie said simply. "She was like you."

"I did a crappy job of that," I said. "I might have done better if I'd known what was going on."

"You know I couldn't tell you."

"So why did she agree to meet you?"

"I was going to take her to you," Julie said. "But he found out." She pointed to Townsend.

"Anything that was done to Phaedra, we did together," he said quietly.

"Not quite," I said. "You raped her. You also were the one who strangled her, I bet."

"I had to make a choice," Townsend said coldly. "Not even Phaedra was worth losing a million dollars and my life. Afterward, I drove her to the desert."

"And you arranged her in a way that would send a message to me."

"Oh, don't think you mattered," he said. "Your exploits merely inspired me. I immediately called the police. I didn't want her body exposed to the elements."

"A compassionate man," I said.

"I didn't intend for it to happen," Julie said. She was different again. She stood up and walked over to Townsend and put her hand on his arm. "But somehow, I know Phaedra understands. She loved me. We loved each other. She wouldn't want me living the way I did."

"You see, Mapstone, it all comes down to money and sex. They're thicker than blood," Townsend said. "I have money and I have Julie. Whatever happened between us, we always wanted to be richer, and we always fucked each other's brains out. Nothing and nobody could ultimately come between that. I hope that doesn't disillusion your bullshit college ardor for her." He raised the gun. "And I am bored with this conversation."

"Did your Julie tell you she slept with me for three nights?" I said hastily. Julie stared at me with a glassy look. Townsend's mouth tightened. "She seemed pretty needy. I didn't hear her calling out your name, Greg."

He jerked his arm away violently and pushed her. "You told me you were through sleeping around, Julie. My health is at stake. And our security."

She looked at him sullenly. "I didn't."

"What else does he know? What did you tell him?"

"Nothing."

He said very quietly, "Lying bitch." And he shot her, the automatic filling the room with a high-pitched, eardrum-bursting blast.

He immediately pointed the gun at me, before I could draw or go to Julie. She was against the wall, sliding down. Blood trickled out around the solar plexus, darkening the center of her light blue blouse. She was staring at me in surprise, moving her mouth silently.

"Don't do it, Mapstone," he yelled. Then: "Tell me what she told you . . . when she fucked you."

I just stared at him with a fool's courage.

He stiffened and then exhaled. "Tell me, and I'll let you go. I mean, I'll just tie you up. That way, I can have time to get away. I'll let you live."

"That's probably what you told Phaedra, too," I said.

"What do you want from me!" he screamed.

"You're the one with the gun pointed at me," I said.

He screwed up his face and lowered the gun a bit. "Let me get my money, and I'll let you live," he said. "I need a partner. You're a smart man."

"And you are a stupid man," I said. "The money's gone. We found the storage locker and Phaedra's car."

His eyes widened. "What the hell are you saying?" He let his elbow drop.

I drew the Colt.

"No!"

The room exploded and something tore into my left shoulder.

I lined up the sights, squeezed the smooth trigger action of the Python, felt the big gun leap in my hand, squeezed it again, and Townsend was instantly blown backward in a cloud of noise and smoke and blood. He collapsed heavily into a lamp, two large holes in his chest, a look of shock and disbelief in eyes that were already dead. The little automatic clattered harmlessly to the floor.

I holstered the Python and knelt before Julie. She was breathing very shallowly and her eyes followed me. The bluest eyes I ever saw. She had lost a lot of blood. Her skin was an ashen color. I started to rise to call for help, but she put her hands on my arms tightly. Tears were running down her face.

"Oh, David," she whispered. "I'm a mess."

My left shoulder was numb. My eardrums were ringing. And I was crying, too. I can't say exactly why.

She pulled herself into me and I held her. "Cold, it's so cold," she said. "David, I'm so cold."

Lindsey and I are not beach people. She does not tan. I become bored too easily. But the gentle San Diego sun feels so good on my shoulder, on the nickel-sized scar just below my collarbone. We lie on a clean, little-used beach I know in the Sunset Cliffs neighborhood, our legs entangling. She is rereading *Anna Karenina*. I am halfway through John Keegan's history of the way battles and war shaped America. It is a good book, and I can almost hold it in my left hand now without pain. The Pacific is the color of Lindsey's eyes, and it is beginning to show the cold restlessness that warns summer is almost over.

The vastness of the ocean reminds me of that night in Sedona, of one of the last things I remembered before passing out. I was found by Deputy Taylor, who summoned help. They carried me out of the cabin to a waiting ambulance, in which I'd be driven to a clearing to meet a medevac helicopter. And the stars—my God, the stars. Billions and billions, uncountable, unimaginable. Pain and shock do strange things. I remember thinking of all the centuries and all the history those pinpoints of light represented. The suns of unimagined civilizations perhaps? Light that had originated when the Declaration of Independence was signed, that had been someone's day and night when Caesar was subduing Gaul. I remember thinking how, back in college, Julie loved for me to drive her into the desert to see the stars. The next thing, I was lying in a hospital bed, groggy. Lindsey was holding my hand tightly, and Peralta was snoring softly in a chair at the foot of the bed.

The next day, Peralta told me what he thought I should know: Townsend was dead, of course. His DNA matched him to Phaedra Riding's murder. The case was closed, "which is more than I can say for the Harquahala murders," Peralta said ruefully. I would have to appear before a board of inquiry, but Peralta assured me it had been a "clean kill." What a strange phrase. I had gone forty years without taking a human life. I wished I could have gone a lifetime.

Sam Larkin confessed to killing Rebecca Stokes. He still claimed it was an accident. His association with Dennis Copeland, a cop killer, would be harder to portray as accidental. Lorie Pope wrote a great Sunday story on the case—hell, I even looked okay without my beard in the photograph. Peralta didn't charge McConnico, who abruptly announced he was retiring from politics.

"Maybe the next governor is Mike Peralta," I said.

Peralta laughed. It was a nice sound.

"You know," I said, "he offered me a professorship if I'd just go along. One old Arizonan to another."

"You have a job," Peralta said.

Now, hard by the sea, Lindsey and I don't talk about all that has happened. We talk about art, literature, jazz, and, of course, history. We read to each other out of a rucksack of books we lug along. We laugh a lot. After we make love, we never talk: The silence and all that has gone before it are too important. And all of this helps. Only occasionally do I think of Julie. Only every now and then do I wake from dreams about her bleeding to death in my arms, so cold, so cold.

I have spent my life with books and ideas. I am a trained historian. But I'll be damned if I understand the devils that destroy human beings, that cause them to destroy themselves. The itches we can't scratch. The dark cells waiting for the right switch to turn on and consume us in a hungry confusion of longing and revenge and rage. Lindsey once asked me if I believe in good and evil, and I do. But I can't bring myself to think of Julie Riding as evil. And that is my failing, for she surely flirted with evil, took it home for a one-night stand, and it moved in for good.

History is an argument without end, as one of my professors used to say. Historians and detectives build cases, believing in the justice of our endeavors. I was trained to sit in academic detachment, take the full measure of time, and formulate arguments that will carry the day in articles, lectures, and books. I expect to know. But detectives don't usually have time on their side. In my new job—or maybe it is my old, old job—there is much I can never know. I am the historian of Rebecca and Phaedra, and I can't say I did a good job.

At night, we walk into Ocean Beach and eat Mexican food and wander through the kitschy shops along Newport Avenue. Lindsey collects postcards and giggles at the tourists, and I adore her more than I should dare.

Just before we came here, I got an E-mail from Patty. She said she was moving back east, to Virginia, and intended to get married again. It didn't bother me. San Diego is no longer a city of demons for me. So maybe some history has been settled.

School has already started, and my internal clock, set by years of teaching, is a bit askew. But no universities are clamoring for me. So I will stay on at the Sheriff's Office as a deputy and a consultant, working the old cases, wearing my star a bit more comfortably, trying not to aggravate Peralta too much. The sheriff, always looking for publicity, wants me to write a history of the department. It's money I'll need.

I never got around to listing the house with a Realtor, and now Lindsey is too fond of it. She can hardly wait to get back and take control of the gardens that Grandmother so loved. I will unpack my books. I will throw the boxes away.

The storms don't come into the city anymore. But maybe they will return someday. There is so much I do not like about Phoenix now: It is too big and too dirty and too dangerous and too hot in the summertime. Behind its dramatic beauty and opulent wealth lie violence and decay made more stark and ugly by the desert. But we grew up together, Phoenix and I. It is the only root, the only touchstone my life has. It is the keeper of my history, as surely as it is the keeper of the Hohokam's. It is my city. It is, for all of this, home.

It is good to be home.